Alexis
gets
frosted

SIMON SPOTLIGHT

An imprint of Simon & Schuster Children's Publishing Division
1230 Avenue of the Americas, New York, New York 10020
Copyright © 2013 by Simon & Schuster, Inc. All rights reserved,
including the right of reproduction in whole or in part in any form.
SIMON SPOTLIGHT and colophon are registered
trademarks of Simon & Schuster, Inc.
Text by Elizabeth Doyle Carey
Chapter header illustrations by Ciara Gay
Designed by Laura Roode
For information about special discounts for bulk purchases, please contact
Simon & Schuster Special Sales
at 1-866-506-1949 or business@simonandschuster.com.
Manufactured in the United States of America 0113 OFF
First Edition 2 4 6 8 10 9 7 5 3 1
ISBN 978-1-4424-6867-2
ISBN 978-1-4424-6868-9 (eBook)
Library of Congress Catalog Card Number 2012953609

CUPCAKE DIARIES

Alexis gets frosted

by coco simon

Simon Spotlight

New York   London   Toronto   Sydney   New Delhi

CHAPTER 1

Back to Reality

Winter break was over and it was back to reality.

I happen to love reality, but my friends weren't so thrilled about it this morning.

Katie still looked half asleep, and Mia was grumpy. Emma was pleasant if a little quiet, but I was raring to go. After all, ten days without school or friends or the Cupcake Club is a long time! By habit, and without even planning it, all of us Cupcake Club members had convened at Mia's locker this morning to catch up before homeroom.

"Why can't it be winter break forever?" Katie was moaning. She leaned against Mia's locker like she couldn't spend the energy to stand up on her own.

"Where is my new assignment notebook?" Mia

wailed, quickly pawing through her tote bag.

I smiled, not wanting to gloat about being all organized and ready. I'd had all my school things laid out since yesterday: my outfit, my books, my pens, and my day planner. Failing to plan is planning to fail, I always say! (But I don't say it out loud too much or my best friends get annoyed.)

"Cupcake Club meeting today after school?" I asked, trying not to sound too cheerful since everyone else was kind of down.

They all looked at me blankly. Then Katie said, "How can you even think that far ahead?"

"We can meet at my house . . . ," I offered. "I have some cool quartz rocks I got on the trip I want to show you."

Mia sighed and slammed her locker shut. "No notebook." Then she looked at me. "Sure, I'll come. It will give me something to look forward to on this horrible first day back," she said.

"Obviously, we'll all be there," said Emma, snapping out of her trance.

"Of course we will," agreed Katie.

Mia was looking carefully at my face.

"What?" I asked. It is kind of annoying to have someone peer at you like that.

"Do you have any balm or cream you can put

on that peeling skin of yours?" she asked.

I'm not much of a cosmetics person, even though I periodically try to get into it. It just seems like too much work, and I hate carrying extra stuff in my bag. I shrugged. "No. Does it look terrible?"

"No . . . just kind of painful," said Mia. "Here." She reached into her tote bag and took out a huge cosmetics case, then she opened it and rummaged for a minute before pulling out a small tube of face cream. "My mom got free samples at the mall. You can keep it till the peeling stops. Just remember to reapply every hour on the hour."

"You know, you really should be more careful about sunscreen on the slopes," said Katie.

"I know, but who would have thought Utah would be so sunny?!" I said. My face had really hurt for days out there, between the sunburn, the windburn, and the dry air.

We reached a turn in the hall and separated for homeroom. I stopped in the bathroom first to apply the cream when Olivia Allen, our resident mean girl, came in. She took one look at me and then began to snicker.

"Does your face hurt? Because it's *killing* me!" she said, and laughed to herself.

"Ha-ha," I said. "Not." I can take a joke, but a

bad one? From someone I don't like? About my appearance? Please.

"What did you do, fall asleep reading a book in the sun?" she said, all serious and fake-concerned.

"No, it's from skiing," I said. I ignored her kind of bratty tone and looked away, busying myself putting the cap back on the cream and stashing it into a pocket of my backpack.

"So, you were reading while skiing? Now that's impressive!" she said sarcastically.

I was confused. "I wasn't reading," I said. "I was skiing."

"Oh, but I know how much you love to geek out on your homework, so I just assumed—"

"Good morning, girls!" said my homeroom teacher, Ms. Dobson, as she went to wash her hands.

I looked at Olivia for a second longer. She was smirking, amused with herself. Why was she going after me all of a sudden? I mean, Sydney Whitman, our former mean girl who moved away to California, was one thing. But Olivia Allen had never before directly attacked me like this. It was surprising and upsetting. My face was flushed, and my ears burned at the tips, which made them even redder, if that was even possible. I kept playing Olivia's comments over in my head, the words "geek out" rattling around like pinballs in a machine. Am I a geek? Is that what people think of me? I was too mortified to even work out what my comeback should have been.

When the warning bell rang to head out to our homerooms, I kept my head turned away from Olivia, hoping she wouldn't say anything else. She must've been satisfied with her morning's work, because she just grabbed her bag and calmly strolled off. I stalled a little to put a good amount of space between us in the hall.

I couldn't wait to tell the other Cupcakers what had happened. Maybe they could help me figure it out.

The morning started off well after that since I had math (which I love) with my favorite teacher, Mr. Donnelly (who rocks). My next class, though, was English, which is not my favorite. We're reading Charles Dickens's book *Great Expectations* and learning about life in Victorian England. Today, Mrs. Carr announced we would each have to complete an independent project with a visual presentation component that shows what it was like to live in Victorian England. *Ugh. Math is so much easier than this,* I thought, heading to gym class.

I was lost in thought as I walked to the locker room. What on Earth would I make? I am not crafty or creative, like Katie, who is obsessed with baking, or Mia, who is obsessed with fashion. When we do Cupcake Club stuff, I am mostly in charge of the business side of things—marketing, invoicing, purchasing, and all the numbers stuff. I knew I'd have to brainstorm for this project with my friends. I just hoped their ideas weren't too wild, because I did not have the skills, patience, or interest to do something over the top.

We didn't have time to talk about it during gym class, so I was still distracted at lunch when I got on line for food, but suddenly, I realized someone had jostled me and cut me in line. I looked up from the silverware rack to see the unmistakable back of Olivia Allen.

"Hey!" I cried out in protest.

Olivia turned back to look at me. "What?" she asked, all innocent.

"You just cut ahead of me!" I sputtered.

Olivia laughed. "Alexis," she said, all fake sweet. "I know you have a hearty appetite, what with all those cupcakes you eat, but can you let other people have a chance at the food too?" Then she turned and kept moving along.

I was speechless. To so rudely and blatantly cut me, and then to insult me on top of it? What a jerk! I fought the urge to bash her over the head with my tray. Luckily for Olivia, she headed off to the salad bar while I stopped for the hot meal. I wished I'd had something clever and mean to say to her to put her in her place. I'd have liked to see her blush and shake for once!

By the time I got my food, I was in a red rage. I sought out my friends and stomped over to join them.

"Uh-oh!" said Emma, spying me. She has been my best friend since we were toddlers, so she can always spot my mad face a mile away. "What happened?"

I slammed my tray down hard on the table. "What happened? What happened? I'll tell you what happened! I hate Olivia Allen, *that's* what happened. She is an evil witch, and she is after me!" I proceeded to tell the others all about Olivia's unwarranted attacks on me so far today. They were appropriately shocked and angry on my behalf, and I began to calm down. By the end of my retelling, I was mostly mad at myself for not coming up with a comeback or beating her down in some way.

"If she was so eager to get her lunch, that line-cutting piggy, then she should have gotten to the cafeteria a little faster!" I snarled.

My friends hooted and clapped. "That's what you should have said to her!" said Mia, laughing. "'Line-cutting piggy'! That's great!"

"I know," I muttered, digging into my fish taco. "I always think of things like that too late. I'm an idiot."

"You're *not* an idiot," said Katie kindly. "You're the opposite. Anyway, would you really want to be the kind of nasty person who always has a sharp comment or comeback ready to go? That's a terrible way to lead your life."

I nodded. She had a point. But still. "Maybe I'd like to be the person who sometimes has a comeback, instead of the person who never does," I said. "Oh, and to make matters worse, I have to do a visual component for my presentation on Victorian England for English! What the heck am I going to make?" I wailed.

Mia clapped her hands. "Ooh. What about a costume? I could help you dress up like a Victorian lady. That would be so much fun! The high, tight waist; the long, full skirts; the lace-up shoes . . . !"

"No, you should do a diorama of, like, people

selling stuff from carts. . . . You know, Victorian business practices!" suggested Emma.

"Hmm. That would be fun to research," I said, already imagining the diorama.

"No, what if you did a diorama out of gingerbread!" said Katie, always thinking about food. "Like a Victorian house, but in gingerbread!"

"Yessss!" cheered Mia and Emma.

"That is totally it!" added Emma.

I thought for a minute. "I think that would be really, really hard, even if it is a cool idea," I said.

"We'll help you!" offered Katie. "It'll be fun!"

"Yeah," Mia chimed.

"Well . . ." It is hard to turn down your three best friends, whom you already know you work well with in the kitchen, when they're offering their help on a horrible project like this.

"And Olivia Allen will be so jealous when she sees it, her eyes will pop out of her head!" said Mia.

Well, that sealed the deal for me!

"Okay!" I agreed. "Thanks, you guys! You really are the best." I pictured Olivia's jaw dropping as I wheeled some massive and spectacular creation into class. All the kids would be oohing and aahing. It would be glorious!

"Hey, wake up, you two dreamers!" Mia laughed.

Katie was also lost in thought. "Wouldn't it be cool to do gingerbread houses from all different eras? Like, imagine a log cabin, *Little House on the Prairie* style. That would be fun to make."

"Oh, I always wished I'd lived then!" said Emma wistfully. "I would have loved those pioneer days."

"Uh-uh, not for me. I'd have liked the nineteen seventies! Just think of the clothes!" Mia sighed. "The whole gypsy-peasant look? I would have totally loved that!"

"I think the nineteen fifties had cool clothes," said Katie. "Those cute Peter Pan collars and the swirly skirts that stick out? I would have looked great in those."

"What about the sixties? All the hippie stuff?" I said.

"We still have a bunch of those kind of clothes from my grandma," said Mia. "My mom saved them because they were so chic."

"It's funny when you see pictures of how your mom used to dress when she was your age, right?" said Emma. "My mom was our age in the eighties, and her clothes were a disaster!"

"I know, but at the time they thought they looked great!" Mia laughed.

I tried to picture my mom back then. We don't

10

have too many pictures of her when she was a kid because she hates clutter. I've seen some at my grandparents' house, but now I was wishing I'd seen more. I made a mental note to ask her when she got home from work tonight.

I looked at my watch. It was time to go. I dreaded seeing Olivia again. My reserves were worn down, and I knew I'd probably burst into tears if she was mean to me again (more from my frustration at not knowing what to say back than anything else!). "Back into battle," I said sadly.

"Come on! You're tough, Becker!" said Emma. "Don't let her get the best of you."

"Yeah, and you've got us to back you up!" said Katie, making a fist so puny, I had to laugh. "What?" she protested. "I'm tough!"

Mia added, "We've got your back, and all she's got is some ragtag band of hand-me-down jerks from Sidney Whitman."

I laughed. "Yeah!"

"Okay, so buck up!" added Mia, rubbing my back supportively. "And remember, fun Cupcake Club meeting at your house today, to look at your new rock thingies."

"Okay. I'm ready! I can do this!" I said, pumping myself up.

And, of course, because I was ready, I didn't run into Olivia again—not for the whole rest of the day! Typical! But still, I couldn't help but wonder what the deal was with Olivia. Why was I suddenly "enemy number one" to her? I forced myself to stop thinking about it and thought about my three smart, beautiful, funny friends instead. Thank goodness for Emma, Mia, and Katie!

CHAPTER 2

Think Pink

We didn't have a whole lot of business in the pipeline, since we were just back from vacation, but we did have our regular client, Mona at The Special Day bridal salon to bake for this Friday, as well as a baby shower coming up the following weekend.

For Mona, we always bake mini cupcakes the width of a quarter, filled, and topped with a burst of frosting. We try to stick to neutral colors and flavors, like white and vanilla, so nothing stains the wedding dresses in her shop.

We needed to buy some supplies, so we voted on a cash disbursement to me, the purchasing agent (I do love titles!), and I would go after school on Thursday to pick up the ingredients we'd need to restock.

As for the baby shower, it was for Emma's little brother's old preschool teacher, Mrs. Horton, so we could be creative. We'd brainstorm now and do test baking at our regular baking session on Friday.

"I'm thinking of those alphabet blocks as a decoration. Like, do the whole alphabet in cupcakes, with each letter frosted on to a little block shape," said Katie.

"Cute!" agreed Emma. "What flavor?"

"It would be cool if we could do a cookies-and-milk flavor somehow, like snack time at school," offered Mia.

We were quiet a minute while we thought through the logistics of that.

"Graham cracker something . . . ," I said.

"With a cream filling?" added Katie.

"Or we could do an apple-cinnamon thing and cream-cheese frosting and then decorate the cupcakes with a little piped red apple with a green fondant stem and leaf? Like, apples for the teacher?" said Mia.

"That's a good one too!" I agreed.

"Yum," said Katie. "Maybe with applesauce in the middle!"

Emma was writing it all down. That way, if I had to get extra supplies for our test baking session on Friday, I'd have all the info I needed.

"Ooh, applesauce," said Emma. "What about baby food cupcakes, since it's a baby shower? Like carrot cake, applesauce cake, sweet potato . . ."

"Broccoli cake?" asked Mia, wrinkling her nose in distaste. "I think we're on the wrong track with that one!"

Emma laughed in agreement, but this was how brainstorming worked. One weird idea can just take off or spark another idea that's actually better. It's like when Emma thought of bacon cupcakes and we all laughed, but they became one of our biggest hits.

"Hey, would you guys mind if I got some gingerbread supplies too, with my own money, of course, while I'm at the store? Then maybe we could get started on it?" I asked.

"Great idea!" said Katie. "I can't wait!"

I smiled, grateful for her support.

"Get started on what?" asked my dad, coming in from the back door and hanging his briefcase and raincoat on a hook.

"Dad! What're you doing home so early?" I asked. I was happy to see him, but it was a surprise. My parents don't usually get home until six or later, and it was only five now.

"Your mom and I have to run to a reception at the new health-care center that my company helped raise money to build. It's just cocktails, so we won't be long, but I want to get in and out as soon as it starts. These charity events are exhausting. I'd rather do the real work than stand around making small talk! Now, what do you girls have cooking?" he asked.

My mom is a health-food nut, so my dad is always scrounging for samples or volunteering to be our tester for things, since he rarely gets baked goods or treats. It's kind of pathetic, but we're grateful to have him as our number-one fan.

"Actually, we're talking about Alexis's class project for English. She's doing a gingerbread house diorama of a Victorian house," Emma said.

"Neat! I can help you if you need anything," my dad said, folding his arms and leaning against the counter. Then he snapped his fingers. "Oh! And also, Mrs. Becker's birthday is coming up, and I'd like to order some cupcakes for her. I've decided we're going to have a little lunch party that day. So, maybe four dozen? We don't want any leftovers. . . ." He grinned.

I smiled at him. "I'm on to you, you know!" I scolded, wagging my finger at him. "Mom doesn't like cupcakes! This is just an excuse so you can have some!"

My dad pretended to be shocked. "Me? What? I don't like cupcakes!" He made a grossed-out face. "Can't stand 'em! No sirree, not me."

We all laughed. Even my friends know how much he loves them.

I shook my head from side to side, still smiling. "What kind?" I asked.

My dad tapped his foot and looked up at the ceiling while he thought. "Well . . . I know the bacon caramel ones are her favorite . . . ," he said, acting all casual.

"Dad! Those are *your* favorite!"

"Me? No way! I told you, I hate cupcakes!"

At this point my friends and I were all laughing really hard when my mom walked in. "What's up?" she asked, smiling as if she wanted in on the joke.

"Dad's just teasing us," I said, then asked slyly, "What are your favorite kinds of cupcakes?"

"Oh, I'm not a big cupcake person . . . ," she said.

At this my friends collapsed into helpless fits of giggles because it was so perfect. My dad pretended to be all exasperated, but he was laughing too.

"She's just kidding because she's actually a

cupcake monster, but she doesn't want you to know it," he said, elbowing her.

My mom said, "Now I am totally confused."

"Really, what kinds of cupcakes do you like?" asked my dad.

My mom thought for a second. "Maybe like a strawberry shortcake kind of thing? Something light and fruity, that's for sure."

My dad raised his eyebrows and gave me a significant nod, like, *Got it?*

I winked at him and gave him a small nod back without her seeing me.

"Why?" asked my mom.

"Just taking a poll," said my dad. "Come on, time to head out."

My mom groaned a little. She didn't want to go either. "See you girls in a bit," she said reluctantly. "You know what? Let me just run and brush my hair. . . ." And she dashed off.

My dad looked down at his shoes and said, really quietly, "And if you felt like making any of those strawberry shortcake cupcakes in caramel, of course . . ."

"Of course!" I said. "All our strawberry shortcake cupcakes come with a side of bacon caramel cupcakes. Right, girls?"

"Absolutely," agreed Mia, smiling.

My dad smiled in relief. "Great!"

"Okay, back to business. This Friday, we have the usual order for Mona, and we're trying the apple-cinnamon and milk-and-cookies cupcakes to see if we should make them for Mrs. Horton's shower next weekend. Then that *same* weekend, for my mom's birthday, we'll do strawberry shortcake and bacon caramel. Two dozen of each." I looked meaningfully at my dad, who nodded, like he had no stake in it whatsoever.

"Now, who wants to help me sketch out a house design for the gingerbread house? We could go look online for images first, and then I could show you my rocks in my room," I said.

Everyone was game, and Mia offered to sketch out the house and figure out the measurements with my help, since I am the math whiz. Katie would figure out how much gingerbread we needed, since she is the baking whiz.

"Have fun, Mr. Becker!" said Emma as we left the kitchen.

"I wish I was staying home and eating cupcakes instead," he said sadly, and we all laughed.

After my parents left, we found some neat images that we printed out, but it was going to be hard to guess the dimensions. Mia started sketching at my desk, and the rest of us turned back to discussing our cupcake jobs as Emma and Katie turned my new quartz geodes over and over in their hands.

"What should we do to make your mom's cupcakes pretty?" asked Katie. "Like, what's she into?"

I was embarrassed for a second because I didn't really know. "Well, she likes things very neat and orderly, so we could make them, like, really perfect looking. . . ."

"And healthy!" said Emma.

I nodded. "Yeah, like low-fat cupcakes with some really light frosting."

"Do you want to decorate or style them in some cute way?" asked Katie.

"Well . . . she's into Sudoku. . . ."

Katie wrinkled her nose in distaste. "Numbers all over our pretty cupcakes?"

I nodded. "I know . . . not everyone loves numbers as much as I do." But what else? "She likes murder mysteries . . . and movies, as long as they're not gross-out comedies."

Katie thought for a second. "Well, maybe, what was she into when she was a kid? Since cupcakes are kind of kiddish."

"You know, I'm not really sure. We don't really

talk about when she was a kid that much."

I could feel Emma looking at me. "You know her favorite color, though, right?" she asked quickly.

"Oh, yes. Pink!" I said, relieved.

Emma did a little clap. "Perfect, then. We'll make the cupcakes pink. They'll be really cute."

Right then I felt grateful to Emma, like she had saved me. But I was still uneasy about my answer. Between not knowing how my mom dressed in the eighties and not being able to come up with what she was into when she was a kid, I felt like I had some homework to do, like I was behind. Everyone else seemed to know all about her mom's childhood, except me.

"Ugh!" Mia crumpled up yet another sheet of paper and then chucked it over her shoulder.

"What's the matter?" I asked.

"It's just really hard to draw something and make it look three dimensional when your only reference is a flat photo."

"I can't even imagine," I agreed since I am not artistic at all.

"I should go," said Emma, making absolutely no move to leave.

"Me too," Katie piped up. But she did stretch and stand up.

"Your rocks are really cool, Alexis," said Emma, handing the geodes back to me.

"Thanks," I said, looking inside at the pink crystals that looked like diamonds.

"I'll keep trying at home," said Mia. "I know I can come up with something."

I smiled at her gratefully. "You're the best. Thank you *so* much."

"It's nothing," she said modestly.

"Your dad is so funny," said Katie as we walked down the stairs. I winced because her dad basically disappeared after her parents got divorced. Katie doesn't talk about it that much, but I know she sees my dad and Emma's dad around all the time and involved, and Mia's dad always makes time to see her, even though he lives in the city and is divorced from Mia's mom. It's got to be hard for Katie.

"He's such a joker," I said, kind of dismissing it. I love my dad so much, but I don't want Katie to feel bad.

"You're lucky," she said.

"Thanks" was all I could say. We had arrived at the back door. "Thanks for everyone's help," I said. And then, because I couldn't let it go, I added, "I'll try to find out some more about what my mom was into when she was a girl. I can't believe I don't even know."

"Pink!" said Emma, and she smiled. "Think pink!"

"Right," I agreed, and smiled back. "She was into pink."

CHAPTER 3

Yessss

That night when my mom came into my room to tuck me in (it sounds so babyish, I hate saying it, but my mom still actually tucks in my covers!), I had to ask.

"Mom, what were you into when you were my age?"

"Me?" It was like she was surprised I was asking and wasn't sure how to answer. "Well . . ." She stared into space for a minute.

"Mom?"

"Oh. Well, I liked ballet. And also my dollhouse."

I propped myself up on one arm. "Your dollhouse? Weren't you a little old for that at my age?"

She winced a little. "Yes. I probably was. But it was so relaxing to work on it, and it was a great project for my mother and me. After Grandpa died when I was eight, she and I moved into a tiny apartment for a few years, just us two. And we worked on this dollhouse and went all over looking for bits and pieces for it. She even bought a kit to electrify it and figured out how to do it all by herself." She smiled at the memory. "It gave us a lot of focus, and I think comforted us, since we missed Dad. Plus, moving from our big beautiful house into the little apartment, we were still able to decorate and shop for our 'house,' but on a much smaller scale. I loved it."

"So why did you get rid of it?" I asked.

My mother looked at me in surprise. "I didn't get rid of it! It's at my mom and Jim's house." My grandmother remarried when my mom was sixteen, and she actually had two more kids, my aunt Margy and my uncle Mike, who are much younger than my mom and lots of fun.

"It is?" I asked, confused. "How come we've never seen it?"

My mother laughed. "I did show it to you girls one time when Dylan was three and you were one, and you two were just grabbing everything and trying to eat it, so I left it there. I'd always meant to bring it here when you girls got old enough to be interested, but you never really were into dolls or anything. Then I kind of forgot about it."

"Can I see it?" I asked.

"Sure," said my mom, shrugging. "I didn't think you were into dollhouses, though."

"I'm not." The one she had bought me when I was eight had sat in a corner of my room untouched for two years before we donated it to the pediatrician's waiting room. "But I'm into knowing more about you when you were a kid!"

With a smile, my mom brushed my hair off my forehead. "I can call Granny and see what her schedule is. I'll find a time to take you over there. Maybe this weekend."

"Thanks," I said, snuggling down into my covers. "Also I want to see pictures of how you dressed in the eighties."

"Oh no! You definitely don't want to see those!" My mom laughed.

"Why?"

"They're awful! Clothes were hideous back then. Except for one little yellow gingham dress I had, with a green pear-shaped patch pocket." She looked all dreamy. "I loved that dress!"

"Hmm. Sounds great." I yawned. "Tell Granny I'd like to see those photos too."

"Why this sudden interest in my past?" asked my mother, turning out the light. She stood in my doorway, just a tall, slender figure backlit by the light from the hall.

"Just interested . . . ," I fibbed. Obviously, I couldn't tell her about the cupcakes, but it was more than that, anyway. It was about my friends knowing way more than I do about their moms and also about wondering how she handled things when she was my age. Like, I wondered if anyone was ever mean to her, like Olivia Allen was to me today. But it was too late to get into that tonight. My mother is all about fixing problems right away, and she'd have the light back on and my dad in here and we'd all be chatting it through, using strategies she learned in her parenting class. It would be misery. I kept my mouth shut. But I made a mental note to find out a little more about what my friends knew about their moms, so I could make sure I was up to speed.

In English the next day, Mrs. Carr went around the room and asked each person to say what they're doing for their project. Lots of kids are doing costumes because, let's face it, it's the easiest. The best student in our class, Donovan Shin, is making a diorama of a Victorian slum. That should be amazing. Olivia is doing a costume of a rich lady of the time, of course. When it got to me, I kind of mumbled; I knew my plan was going to be hard to do, and I almost hated committing to it by saying it out loud.

"A diorama," I said quietly.

"A diorama?" asked Mrs. Carr, confirming she'd heard me right.

I nodded. "Of a house," I added miserably.

"I'm sure it will be lovely," said Mrs. Carr with a smile. "Next?"

I spaced out, hoping Mia had come up with some kind of blueprint last night. I hadn't seen her yet today to ask.

Suddenly, Olivia leaned forward from where she was sitting diagonally behind me and said, "I'm surprised you didn't figure out a way to bake something fattening and call it a project."

I turned around in shock, feeling like I'd been slapped and also mortified because, of course, I am baking something for the project.

"What?" was all I could think to say. Brilliant, as usual.

"Olivia, do you have a comment you'd like to share with the class?" asked Mrs. Carr loudly.

She became my favorite teacher right then, even though I still hate English.

Olivia blushed a little at being called out, which was awesome!

"N-no," she stammered. "I was just saying I'd hoped Alexis would be baking a treat for us since she's such a good baker and all." She shifted in her seat uncomfortably, and I turned around to look at Mrs. Carr and shake my head a little, like, *No, that is not what she said*. Mrs. Carr caught my gist.

"Let's keep our comments about other people's plans to a minimum, shall we?" suggested Mrs. Carr.

I turned for one last triumphant look at Olivia, and she was glaring at me but now with a full blush on her face. But my moment of victory passed as it suddenly sank in that Olivia would only be meaner to me now, just to get back at me. I shrank down in my chair and stared straight ahead, bracing myself for the worst.

What had I ever done to Olivia to deserve this abuse? It was so out of the blue! Like she'd come back from the break and decided she hated me. Ugh. The class couldn't pass fast enough now! I had to get out of there.

A few minutes later, when Mrs. Carr's back was to the class, I felt a scratching on the back of my arm. I looked down and it was a note, being passed from Maggie, behind me to my left. Maggie used to hang around with Sydney Whitman in the Popular Girls Club. When Sydney moved away, the club was renamed the Best Friends Club, and Olivia started hanging out with Maggie and Bella. The weird thing about this group of girls, the Best Friends Club, is that on their own, they're not all that bad—usually. It's only when they're together that they're awful.

Glancing up at Mrs. Carr to make sure I was safe, I quickly reached back to snatch the note. Then casually, over the course of a few minutes, I slowly opened it up without making any noise, and read what it said:

You should be careful what you say about people if you don't want them to get angry at you.

What? Olivia was angry at me? Because I said something about her? I couldn't even begin to imagine what it would be. And how could something I said hurt someone as powerful as Olivia Allen? Lowly old me?

Now I was stressed.

I didn't write a return note, and as soon as the class was over, I flew out the door to gym class without looking back.

After gym though, I still didn't even want to go to lunch and potentially face her there, too. I felt like I was on the run, like a character on a TV show. I grabbed a sandwich and then told my friends I had a meeting of the Future Business Leaders of America, and I took off to eat my lunch alone in the math lab. It was depressing, but at least I felt safe. After school I commandoed out of the building and raced home without running into anyone. It was like I was in the witness protection program.

At home I IM'd my BFFs to say I wasn't feeling well, and even though I felt bad for lying, I knew it would buy me some time alone. I just had to figure out what I'd said about Olivia, and in the meantime, how to stay the heck away from her.

To distract myself, I really focused on my homework and did a great job, and I made a little headway on a spreadsheet I'm working on for the CC that details the specific quantities of ingredients needed for each of our standard cupcake designs.

At six fifteen, my mom dashed by with a quick hello as she changed out of her work clothes and went into the kitchen to make one of her super-healthy dinners for us. I was just glad to be left alone.

When they called me down for dinner, I went, but I was still distracted by the drama of my day.

As soon as I sat down, my older sister, Dylan, said, "I thought you were sick."

"What?" I could feel my cheeks pinken into a blush.

"I saw Emma at the library a little while ago, and she said you'd rushed home because you didn't feel well."

My mom put down her fork. "What's the matter, Lexi? Do you have a fever? Your cheeks are all pink."

She stood up and came over to press her lips to my forehead, which is the annoying and mortifying way she checks to see if we're feverish. (For some reason my mom is always obsessing that we might have fevers. Always has, always will, for reasons unknown.) I tried to squirm away, but she had me in a tight grip.

"No, no fever," she said, returning to her seat, visibly relaxed. She picked her fork back up and began eating again. "What is it? Your allergies?"

"Yeah," I said.

"'Yeah'?" my mom repeated, and raised her eyebrows a little at me. She hates when we use that word. "There's an *s* on the end of that word, correct?"

"Yessss," I corrected myself. "Just itchy eyes and a runny nose and stuff." I was thrilled for the excuse she'd thrown me, even though it wasn't nice of me to fib to my parents.

"It's going to be a bad year for allergies. All this dryness. No snow this year to fill up the groundwater," said my dad.

"I know. It was the worst skiing year on record," agreed my mom. "Those poor ski-resort owners. You know the Campbells canceled their trip. . . ."

I tuned out what she was saying as something in my mind began buzzing. Snow. Skiing. Ski resorts . . . OMG!

"Oh no!" I moaned out loud without meaning to.

"Sweetheart!" cried my mother. "What is it?" She looked at me all wide-eyed and scared.

"Oh, nothing. Sorry." I felt sheepish. "Just something I forgot to bring home for homework. I have to call Emma."

Everyone looked at me suspiciously. Not only am I a bad liar but I'd thought up a bad lie. I'd never forgotten something I needed in all of my life. I am the most organized person I know!

"Oookay," my mom said skeptically.

I started to stand up to call Emma, and my father said, "Not right now, young lady. It's dinnertime." And he pointed back to my chair.

"Sorry," I said. Then I wolfed down the rest of my dinner, and asked to clear my plate and be excused.

"Wait!" said my mom. "One thing I forgot to tell you before you go! Granny said we could come out Saturday morning to see the dollhouse and all the photos. She's thrilled to get things organized and lay them all out for you." My mom smiled.

"Thanks, Mom," I said. I tried to muster up some excitement as I scraped my plate into the disposal, but all I could feel right now was dread.

"Wait, what's all this about Granny?" asked Dylan, and I left my mother to explain. Dylan would hate to miss out on anything with our grandmother because she gives us great old things all the time, like clothes and records and stuff, which Dylan loves.

I took the stairs up two at a time and grabbed the cordless phone from the hall table as I sprinted by. Inside my room I frantically dialed Emma's number without even stopping to think what I usually think, which is that my crush—her brother Matt—might answer the phone. Which he didn't, luckily.

"Alexis?"

I love caller ID.

"Thank goodness you answered. I figured it all out."

"Wait, the gingerbread house?"

I could hear the confusion in Emma's voice.

"No! Olivia Allen!"

"Oh. What?"

"I know why she's after me. Remember when we were in the hall talking the day we got out for break about my ski trip? And Maggie and Bella were there? And Maggie was asking where we were going and everything, and she said something about how Olivia used to be, like, a professional skier in the Alps or something?"

"Yeah . . ."

(*Yessss!* I thought, channeling my mom, but I didn't say it!) "Well, remember how Maggie said something that wasn't really nice about Olivia, and we were kind of surprised because we thought they were BFFs?"

"Oh yeah! Something about how it always has to be the best with Olivia or whatever?"

"Right!" I agreed, feeling relief she remembered too. "So then I said some joke about, 'Well, she probably thinks she's an Olympic skier, but she's really one of those people who just wears the outfits and sits in the lodge all day.' Remember that?"

"Uh-huh," agreed Emma, giggling. "It's true!"

"Well, I was just trying to make Maggie feel better, because she was obviously annoyed at Olivia for some reason, and I thought I'd just chime in. But then I said something like, 'I can't stand those kind of posers!' or something."

"Oh," said Emma, now not giggling.

"Uh-huh. And I think Maggie told her."

"That traitor! You were just trying to make her feel better."

"Well, all I did was make myself feel worse!"

"What can we do?" asked Emma.

I loved that she said "we"! "I don't know. But you're the best," I said.

"Yeah, but you're still number one on Olivia's hit list."

"Yessss," I agreed sadly. "Yessss."

CHAPTER 4

Quack

I resolved to confront Maggie first and to find out why she had ratted me out to Olivia. My nerves wavered, though, when I saw her walking in the hall with Callie. They were all dressed up, looking stylish and chatting intently, and I was too scared to interrupt them as they sailed by, oblivious to my existence.

My luck was with me, though, because I ran into Maggie in the bathroom just before homeroom.

"Uh, Maggie?" I started, approaching her at the sink. My voice was kind of shaky. So not the image I wanted to project! I cleared my throat and then tried to establish some presence and poise, as if I were delivering a business presentation.

"Hi," she said in kind of an oh-it's-just-you tone of voice. She peered at herself in the mirror and took out her makeup case.

"Listen, I just . . . I'm wondering . . . Why did you tell Olivia that dumb joke I made about her and skiing?"

Maggie turned and looked at me blankly. "What?" she asked.

"You know, the note you passed me yesterday. About being careful about what I say about people?"

"Yes, but it wasn't me who told her. It was Bella." Her face darkened, and she turned back to the mirror. "She said it was both of us—you and I—talking about Olivia. She's a total tattletale, just trying to suck up to Olivia."

Isn't that what you do? I wanted to ask, but I didn't think the timing was quite right.

"So, wait . . . Why isn't Olivia mad at you too?"

"She was," said Maggie, kissing her lips together to spread her clear lip gloss. She studied herself critically, took out a brush, and began to run it through her hair.

This was like pulling teeth! Now exasperated rather than intimidated, I said, "So why isn't she mad at *you* anymore?"

Maggie put her brush away, zipped her case shut, and stowed it into her bag. "Because I apologized," she said briskly. And she turned on her heel and left me there, gaping.

Great, I thought. *Now I have to apologize to Olivia?* I couldn't even picture it. And since she'd been so mean to me, part of me didn't even want to. Like, why should I be nice and kiss up to her, after all the mean stuff she's said this week? She should apologize to me!

I felt that horrible dread in my stomach that I'd been feeling the past two days, ever since Olivia started being mean to me. I looked in the mirror Maggie had just vacated and saw my pale face, worried eyes, and set jaw. I looked scared and unhappy.

I took a deep breath and rearranged my features. Then, looking over my shoulder to make sure no one was around to see, I smiled at myself. I read in some self-improvement manual of Dylan's that if you smile, it tricks your body into thinking you're happy. But it wasn't working. I smiled harder. Still nothing.

Sighing, I frowned and felt better.

Well, at least I had a game face. Maybe that would scare Olivia away.

And I had math right after homeroom. That would be fun.

Except that it wasn't.

In math class, Mr. Donnelly announced we'd be merging with the other two sections to form teams for the school's math rally. He said we've move around classrooms for the next couple of days, and then he read the list of who was on which team.

See if you can guess who was on mine.

The good news was I got to stay in my classroom. The bad news was that Olivia came in and sat one row away from me. When Mr. Donnelly handed out the sheets of practice problems for us to work on, he broke us into groups of four or five kids and had us all move our desks into little circles, so we could talk. That left me staring right at Olivia Allen. Ugh.

Kids were chatting about their weekend plans when Olivia asked loudly, "Alexis, do you do anything besides math homework and baking on the weekends?"

All the other kids turned to listen, because they could tell by her tone of voice that something was brewing. Kids love a good drama. But I didn't want to be the star of it.

I took a deep breath and then I looked her in the eyes and replied, "It depends on what my boyfriend is doing. He's in high school." I had no idea how I came up with that! I felt my face turn red with the lie, but I also had to hide my grin. It was the first time I'd had any sort of comeback for her, and I was thrilled, even if it was a fib. *Maybe if you practice enough, you can get kind of good at comebacks,* I thought.

I looked down at Mr. Donnelly's practice sheet as if to say, *This conversation is finished.* I could feel the other kids watching Olivia to see what she would come up with next, but seconds passed, and she didn't say anything. I was so proud of myself, I wanted to burst!

Finally, she said, "Good luck with that. I think it's illegal."

I shrugged without looking up, like, *Who cares what you think?* I turned to this kid, Aubrey Peterson, next to me and asked if he wanted to quiz me. I felt light-headed, like I was floating. It must've been the adrenaline from my fear, but I was pleased with myself. By the end of class she hadn't said another word to me and I had come back down to Earth.

Maybe I'd made things worse in the long run

by winning the battle but not the war. I mean, how was I going to come up with a boyfriend in high school? But it didn't matter. It had felt great. And even if she threw worse stuff at me now, thinking I was tougher than I looked, it didn't matter. I'd always savor my first victory.

At home in bed that night, I mentally replayed the whole scene in math class. I was proud of myself for my bravery and my cleverness. But as the minutes ticked by in the dark, my pride shrank and my fear grew. I was ashamed of myself for lying and being mean, and I knew my fighting back had only fanned the flames of Olivia's anger. I dreaded the wildfire I was sure to face from her soon.

On Thursday I snuck around school like a hunted animal, peering around corners and slinking down halls. I skipped lunch with my friends again and ate alone, then at dismissal, I raced out of there and literally ran home. I was relieved I'd avoided Olivia again, but it was no way to live.

By dinner I was exhausted. I guess I didn't say much, or maybe it was obvious I was tired and stressed, because my mom came into my room after she did the dishes and sat on my bed.

"What's up?" she asked.

I wasn't sure I wanted to get into it with her. As I said, she can get a little too intense about problem-solving sometimes. I sighed.

Then I spilled the beans. All of them.

"Wow," said my mom. "I'm sorry you've been going through all this. I wish you'd told me."

"Yes, but it's just been kind of snowballing, getting bigger and bigger. I didn't realize it was my new way of life."

My mom was looking thoughtful. "You know, there was a mean girl in my class when I was your age. . . ."

"I know. Susan! You always tell us about her!" I rolled my eyes.

My mom smiled. "Well, she comes in handy in a lot of lessons. Anyway, mean people take a lot of energy, and it's not worth it. And they can make you act mean too, just to protect yourself. That can be a terrible feeling, because then you're losing yourself. It sounds like that's what happened yesterday."

I winced, thinking of how proud I'd been of my comeback yesterday but how bad it had made me feel later.

"You know, most of the Olivias in the world

are really just insecure, and their mean streak comes from being hurt."

I rolled my eyes again. "Excuses, excuses," I said. "Everyone is insecure, Mom!"

She nodded. "Come on, though. Olivia is obviously hurt. And you were mean in what you said about her and skiing. Think of it this way: You're the one who's lived here all your life, and you're the one with the tight-knit group of friends, who really knows yourself and has a strong identity and a good reputation in the school, right? And then you insult her behind her back, questioning her claims about her athletic abilities, all when she's new to the school and trying to establish herself. How do you think that makes her feel?"

It was weird to flip the problem on its head like that, but it was true, when you looked at it from the other side. I felt bad now.

"I guess she's probably hurt," I said, ashamed.

My mom sighed. "You did start this, Alexis, and I didn't raise you to be a mean girl. But I *really* didn't raise you to be a victim, which is what Olivia's retaliation is turning you into. Right?"

I nodded.

"Look, you don't want to waste your time feeling bad, or being mean or hiding. Those are all negative states. You need to apologize to Olivia and to get that out of the way. I think it will clear the air with her, and it will take care of your conscience. No more sleepless nights!" she said.

I nodded again. Reluctantly. I dreaded apologizing. How soon would I have to do it? I wondered. And where would I do it? And what would I say? Ugh.

My mom prodded me out of my daydream. "So, you'll get the ball rolling with an apology and let me know what happens? I support you all the way, sweetheart." She leaned over and gave me a kiss and a hug. "Now we'd better get to the store to stock up on those ingredients you need for tomorrow."

"Oh right. Hey, Mom," I said. "What ever happened with Susan? I mean, did she stop being mean to you?"

Standing in the doorway now, my mom paused. "As you know from other stories, she was awful, and she had a crowd who hung on everything she said. She picked on me. So one day I just couldn't take it anymore. I screwed up my courage, and I confronted her and told her that I didn't appreciate it, but that, really, her behavior had no effect on me whatsoever. I asked why I was so fascinating to her that she was spending so much time watching and commenting on what I was doing."

I gasped. "What happened?"

"Well, I guess Susan found me less interesting after that. We stayed away from each other, but she never singled me out again."

"Huh," I said.

"Something to think about," Mom said. "But don't think about it too much, Alexis. You are great the way you are. You have wonderful friends, a family who loves you, and one big, bad Olivia shouldn't get in the way of any of that. You need to act like a duck."

I had to smile. It's one of my mom's favorite things to say when Dylan or I get ruffled: Act like a duck and let it roll off your back.

"Quack!" I said, and my mom quacked back, and grinned.

Of course I didn't see Olivia at all the next day. I'm not sure if she was even at school. But I marched around bravely, my head held high, ready for action, ready to change my situation.

At lunch I sat front and center with the Cupcakers, and even though we saw Bella, Maggie, and Callie, there was no Olivia. Typical. Just when I have my nerve up, she's nowhere to be found.

We chatted about our baking session later in the day and the fact that I'd made no progress on my diorama plans, but I promised to figure something out over the weekend. We only had the coming week and weekend to work on it, so if I didn't figure it out now, I was sunk.

"I guess I could always ask Mrs. Carr if I can switch to a costume," I said glumly.

"Yay!" said Mia, but Katie gave her a dirty look that silenced her.

"I'll work on it too, Alexis," said Katie. "It's too cool of an idea to bag. You know, let's at least try to make some gingerbread this afternoon and see how hard it is to work with. We're not giving in to costumes yet!"

"Thanks."

"By the way, speaking of costumes," said Mia. "I was talking to my mom about the eighties clothes and everything, and I found out she was the wardrobe mistress for the school productions all through middle school and high school! Isn't that typical?!"

We all laughed, and Emma said, "Guess what I found out about my mom? She played the flute! Just like me! Except she quit, and she always regretted it, and that's why she wanted me to play."

Katie said, "How about this: My mom was

allergic to eggs and milk when she was a kid, and she never even ate a cupcake until she was fifteen!"

We were all still laughing. I didn't have much to add. "I'm going to my grandma's tomorrow to see some old photos of my mom and her dollhouse from when she was a kid."

"Cool! I love dollhouses!" said Katie.

"I'll take a picture and then e-mail it to you," I promised.

We were quiet for a minute, picturing everyone's moms as kids. Then Emma snapped her fingers. "Hey! You know what could be really cool? If we did a time capsule. We could put in tons of things about us and even stuff about our moms. Then we'll bury it for our kids!"

"That's a great idea!" I said, and everyone agreed.

We spent the rest of the meal brainstorming about what to put in and how to get it, and lunch flew by. We planned to meet up again later at Emma's to bake and finish our plan.

CHAPTER 5

House Hunting

After school I stopped off at home to pick up some supplies, then headed over to Emma's, but not without taking a few minutes to brush my hair, change out of my school clothes and into something cuter, and put on just a tiny dab of lip gloss and some earrings. Hey, you never know who could be over at the Taylors', with all those cute brothers of hers. But hopefully the love of my life, Matt Taylor, would show up at some point.

At Emma's, we set up three workstations. We only need one person to make Mona's minis since we could all do it with our eyes closed at this point. Emma did that since Mona is her special friend. Mia took on the baby shower samples. She had the two different recipes to try—apple cinnamon and milk and cookies—and Katie and I played around with the gingerbread.

It was easy enough to make the dough, but the hard part was getting the sheets of baked gingerbread just right. Katie had found an amazing website that had recipes along with instructions on how to build elaborate gingerbread houses. We had to figure out what mine would look like and then we could start making templates for the pieces.

The back door slammed and my heart leaped. Was it Matt?

"Hey, Cupcakers," greeted Matt, dumping his gear in his locker at the back door. "Smells like Christmas in here!"

Yes! It was him! I willed myself not to blush.

"It's because we're making apple-cinnamon cupcakes for a job and a gingerbread mansion for Alexis's class project," Mia said.

Matt went to Mia's side to inspect the cupcakes, then he looked at me. "Alexis's class project? Alexis has everyone working for her now?" he teased. "Why am I not surprised by that?"

And the blush I'd been fighting rose up my neck and cheeks as I giggled.

"She's the CEO!" said Mia.

"In training!" I protested.

Matt came over to inspect the printed ginger-bread house instructions and our dough. "This looks hard!" he said.

"I know," I agreed glumly.

He looked at me. "Couldn't you do something easier for your class project? Like a costume or something?"

"That's what I said!" singsonged Mia.

I groaned and put my head in my hands.

"Run along, now, Matthew! You're scaring her!" said Katie, shooing him away.

He laughed, grabbed an apple and a pear from the fruit bowl on the counter, and headed up to his room. "Let me know if you need any computer help!" he called back over his shoulder.

"Thanks," I replied listlessly.

Katie was reading the directions aloud now. "We need to roll the dough out to a quarter-inch in thickness and then cut it into the shapes we need. I'll cut four equal squares for walls, and we can put aside two to add windows and another to add a door, okay?"

I watched her work and noticed how easily it came to her. Her hands did what she wanted them to, and things turned out beautiful looking as well as delicious.

Katie slid the tray into the oven to bake and then continued poring over the instructions. It wasn't that interesting to me, and I felt bad, like Katie was doing all the work for me. But she did seem to be enjoying it. And it had been her idea in the first place.

I went to check on Mia's progress, and things were looking good. The cakes were baking and smelling great, and she was whipping up two kinds of frosting. The one for the apple-cinnamon cakes would be cream cheese, with caramelized apple chunks on top, and the other was a fluffy vanilla cream, for the cookie cakes. I sampled both and liked the cream-cheese one better.

"You could use this with any kind of fruit, you know," said Mia, looking around the kitchen. "Caramelized bananas would be delicious. Pear. Even pineapple."

"Yum," I agreed. The word "pear" stuck in my mind for a minute, and then I realized why. My mom's dress! Maybe we should do a pear cupcake for her! And we could cover a platter in yellow-and-white gingham fabric or paper and then arrange the cakes in a pear shape; maybe pipe little green pears on top of each one! That could be cute.

I checked on Emma and Mona's minis. She

was ready to frost, so I jumped in and helped. We finished quickly, and then it was time for my gingerbread to come out.

Everyone gathered around to watch Katie handle the bread. First, she lifted the walls off the tray and then set them to cool on a wire rack for just a minute. Then, one at a time, she trimmed them to make the edges perfect (gingerbread expands a lot in the oven), and then she popped the scored areas out with a knife. The finished product looked great.

While they cooled, she readied her supplies. She had made a bowl of icing, which would hold everything together. It was white, but we could dye it any color we wanted when we did our real project. She also had a cardboard base where she'd drawn the outline of the house, like a blueprint. In the middle of the outline she set two unopened soup cans. The cans would prop the walls up while the icing dried, so they wouldn't fall over.

"Katie, you've thought of everything! Thanks!" I cried.

Katie smiled modestly. "I think this is really fun. Maybe if we get good at it, we could start a sideline in fancy gingerbread houses!"

"We could charge a lot of money for them," remarked Mia.

"I'll have to run the numbers on that, because they're pretty labor intensive," I added.

"What does that mean?" asked Emma.

"It means it takes a lot of hours to build them, and at a certain point, it's not worth it. Time is money."

"But you're the one who always says, 'If you're going to hang out with your best friends, you might as well be making money while you're doing it,'" Emma pointed out.

I grinned. "I'm glad someone's listening!"

"Oh please," said Mia, laughing. "We all know your mottoes by heart. 'Failing to plan is planning to fail!'" she said in a chipper voice.

"'Business first!'" cried Katie.

"'Knowledge is power!'" added Emma, laughing.

"All right, stop! This is embarrassing!" I said. My face was red, but it was funny, and it felt good to have friends who knew me so well. I looked over my shoulder. I just didn't want Matt to hear them!

"We have to make sure we get all those little Alexis quotes into the time capsule," said Emma.

I rolled my eyes.

"You *are* a character, Alexis," said Mia, shaking her head and still laughing.

"Thanks. I think," I said.

Katie deemed the walls sufficiently cool, and we began assembling them. It wasn't easy. The icing was slippery, and the walls were surprisingly heavy, and it took a little getting used to. Katie thickened up the icing with more confectioners' sugar, so it was a little pastier (I wouldn't have thought of that but was glad she did). That did the trick.

We very quickly had the four walls standing, and with the little door and windows cut out, it looked really cute.

"So once it's built, how long do you wait to decorate it?" I asked.

"Overnight," replied Katie.

I did some calculations. "We'd have to bake Tuesday, build Wednesday, decorate Thursday. Which means I need the plans ready by Tuesday morning."

"Monday," corrected Katie. "Because you'd need to print them out, then cut them out so they can be traced, and I bet that takes a while. Don't forget, you'll also need a good shopping trip to get all the supplies. We'll probably need a trip to the baking store at the mall. Maybe this weekend."

I smiled at her. That place was heaven for Katie, and she didn't get to go too often. Again, I was grateful for her use of the word "we."

"Okay. I guess we have our work cut out for me," I joked.

"We sure do!" agreed Katie.

We finished and then packed Mona's cupcakes for delivery the next morning. Then we called Matt down for a taste test of the two kinds of sample cupcakes (my idea). He was happy to oblige.

The cookies and milk was first, and he liked it, but didn't rave.

The second he bit into the apple-cinnamon one, though, it was the clear winner.

"Wow. Oh! This one is off-the-chart good!" he said with his mouth full. "It's insane! You've got to make these." He crammed the rest of the cake into his mouth. "Can I have another?" he asked with his mouth full, gesturing toward the plate.

"Please?" prompted Emma, exasperated. Her brothers drive her crazy.

I gladly handed him another, "please" or no "please." It was fun to see someone enjoy our cupcakes this much, and it was extra special that it was Matt, whom I secretly love, but also because he's helped us out so many times. He's a big supporter of the Cupcake Club, which I appreciate.

"How's the house?" he asked, turning to look at it.

"Pretty good!" I said. "Katie's a whiz!"

Katie blushed modestly.

"The hard part's going to be making the blueprints or templates or whatever," I said.

Matt nodded, swallowing his last bite. "I can help you with that," he offered.

"Really?"

"Sure, no prob," he said. "I have a CAD program we can run. It will be easy."

"Okay! Thanks! What's CAD?"

"Computer-aided design. It turns your ideas into blueprints."

"Cool."

"I'll just need the design," he said.

"Right," I agreed.

"You do have the design, right?" he prompted.

"Well . . . not exactly," I admitted.

"But she will very soon!" Katie said brightly. "Right?"

"Right," I repeated miserably.

"Uh-oh!" said Matt.

❧

Trudging home from Emma's, I tried to think of how I could get some kind of plans or measurements together for the gingerbread house. I'd looked online for hours but couldn't find anything close to what I was hoping. There had been a few kinds of houses that looked good, but they were so complicated—so professional—I couldn't begin to even *think* about taking them on.

I'd have to ask my parents at dinner, to see if they had any ideas.

When my mom called me to come in for dinner at seven, I was lying on the sofa in the den (which is also my mom's home office), watching my favorite show, *Celebrity Ballroom*, and sorting paper clips by color from a big bin into a small tackle box. It was very relaxing. I almost couldn't pry myself away.

At the table, I must've sighed one too many times, because my mom stopped eating and then looked at me carefully. "What's up, sweetheart?" she asked.

Dylan was out, so my mom and dad and I could speak freely without worrying about Dylan butting in or ragging on me.

I knew my mom was assuming this had to do with Olivia, and I was glad to say it didn't. "It's my class project," I said morosely. "We have to do a presentation with a visual component on Victorian times for English class."

"Well, what are you doing?"

"A Victorian house made out of gingerbread," I said.

My mom and dad both burst out laughing.

"Sorry, honey," said my dad. "It's just . . . Of all of a parent's worst nightmares . . . The class project thing . . . And to have it be something so intense like that. It's just funny to us."

"Like when Dylly had to do that Alaska project!" My mom laughed.

"And she insisted on making an igloo out of sugar cubes!" added my dad, howling.

"A huge igloo!" My mom roared with laughter. "Two thousand sugar cubes!"

"And the glue!" They were gasping with laughter now.

"I'm glad you think this is funny," I said, without even cracking a smile.

"Wait, is this something the teacher assigned or you picked?" asked my dad, mopping his eyes with his napkin.

"Well, I kind of picked it. It was Katie's idea."

"Can you change it?" asked my mom hopefully.

I shook my head, picturing Olivia's face when I brought in my fantastic creation. No way would I change now.

"You couldn't do a costume?" she asked.

I made an aggravated sound. I wished they would ban the word "costume" from the English language for a week!

"And how far have you gotten?" asked my dad.

I shrugged. "Nowhere."

"And when's it due?" asked my mom.

"Next Friday," I said.

"At least it's not due tomorrow!" remarked my dad, and the two of them got to hysterically laughing again.

I stood up. "Until you two can control yourselves, I will be leaving the table. Thank you for dinner," I said.

"No, stay, stay. We're sorry, sweetheart. We won't laugh again," my dad replied.

"We promise," added my mom.

They could barely suppress their smiles, but I sat back down again, anyway. *How could two individuals be so annoying?* I wondered.

"So what's the first step?" asked my dad.

I sighed heavily. I could barely describe it. "I need to find a Victorian house to use as a model for the gingerbread house, so we can put the measurements into a CAD program and create templates for the gingerbread."

"Oookaay . . . ," said my dad, thinking.

My mom bit her lip, staring into space.

"There's a Victorian out on Route 20," said my dad to my mom. "You know the one?"

She nodded, but she was still distracted.

"Maybe we could go knock on their door, ask if we could measure?" He shrugged.

"No. I've got it!" My mom snapped her fingers, grinning. "I have *got* it!"

"What?" my dad and I asked in surprise.

"My old dollhouse! The one we're going to see at Granny's tomorrow! It's a Victorian!" She folded her arms in triumph. "We'll just measure that!"

"Oh, Mom!" I cried, and I threw my arms around her neck. "Yay!"

"Let the games begin!" said my dad.

CHAPTER 6

The Little House

The trip to my grandmother's only takes about an hour. It's too bad we don't go more often, but with everything we have going on, it's hard to find the time to get out there. Usually she just comes to us, which she says she loves, because she gets to see us "in our own environment."

But my granny's house is really neat. It's old and it rambles. It's not supertall; the second story has only two of the bedrooms in it, and both are kind of in the eaves, with little dormer windows bumped out, and window seats. But there have been so many additions to the back of the house over the last two hundred years that it twists and turns and teems with hidden nooks and crannies. It's great for hide-and-seek.

As it turned out, Dylan had cheerleading practice and couldn't come. (I think she never really had any interest in coming—she just wanted to be invited.) So it was just my mom and I who went, which was better, anyway. When we got there, my granny and granddad (who isn't really my granddad, but I call him that because he's the only one I've ever known) were eagerly waiting for us. He had already gone to the Milburn Deli and bought sandwiches, coleslaw, and hard-boiled eggs, plus Cokes and chips and peanut butter Kandy Kakes for dessert, which we always have when we visit. It's junk food heaven (kind of my mom's worst nightmare!) and delicious.

First, we ate at the kitchen table, and afterward, while Granddad cleaned up, Granny, Mom, and I headed into the dining room to look at all the photos they'd laid out for us. I was dying to see the dollhouse, but I didn't want to seem pushy, so I kept my mouth shut for the moment.

"Lexi, look at this adorable picture of your mom," said Granny, holding out a photo. I took it and carefully inspected it, surprised by what I saw. It was my mom in the now-famous pear dress, but what surprised me was how messy she looked. My mom is always as neat as a pin—not a hair out of place, her clothes perfect, everything under control. But here, in the pear dress, her hair was wild and her knees were dirty, and one sock was falling down, and on the other foot, her shoelace was untied. And she had a big red mustache, like she'd been drinking red juice.

"Mom!" I said. "I can't believe it! Is this really you?" I held the photo toward her. She took it and looked, then she laughed.

"What a mess I was!" she said.

My granny peered over her shoulder. "You were adorable. I still have that dress somewhere. I just couldn't put my hands on it for today. I'll keep looking."

I took back the photo and then studied it again: my mom's wild looping curls (the same ones she carefully blow-dries straight every day), her dirty face (the one that now has always-perfect makeup on it), her messy outfit (ahem).

"What happened?" I asked. "When did you get so neat?"

My mom laughed a little, like she was embarrassed, but my granny said, "After your granddad died—your grandfather Jack, I mean—your mom grew up a lot, and quickly."

"I had to!" she protested.

My granny chuckled. "Well, I don't know about that. It wasn't like you didn't have anyone to look after you. You still had me!"

"I know, but I didn't want to make any trouble or more work for you," said my mom. "And you always had that motto. . . ."

My granny waved her hand, laughing. "Oh please! I only said that a few times."

"What? No! You said it every day!" protested my mom.

Now this was fascinating stuff. They sounded like me and my mom. Or maybe more like Dylan and my mom.

"What was the motto?" I asked.

"'You can't lay down and die just because he did,'" said my mom. "That's what she always said."

My granny gave an exasperated huff. "I only said it a few times. And I was saying it more for myself than for you." She turned to me. "Your mother was a wild and carefree child, but when her dad died, she became very serious and hard on herself. She felt she had to be perfect and look perfect, so no one would feel sorry for her. It broke my heart. She already was perfect." My granny reached over and gave my mom a hug.

Now my mom was kind of teary. Wow. This

65

was heavy stuff. It would definitely not be going in the time capsule!

"Oookaay . . . ," I said. "Awk-ward!"

They laughed.

"Sorry, sweetheart," said my mom, grabbing a Kleenex out of her bag and then blowing her nose.

"All right, who wants to see the dollhouse?!" my granddad boomed, coming into the room, clueless to all the girlie drama going on.

"Me!" I yelled, relieved to be getting out of there. I am so not one for crying or being all huggy or anything. Plus, I was dying to see if this little house would solve all my problems.

"Let's go, champ!" said my granddad.

In the finished basement rec room, the dollhouse was set out on a waist-high table, with a sheet over it. My granddad said, "Close your eyes. I want you to get the full effect, just at first."

So I closed my eyes, and I could hear him rustling, then I heard a click and another click, and when he told me to open my eyes, the overhead lights were out, but the dollhouse was lit up and glowing like a real little home!

"*Oh!*" I gasped, and rushed across the room to see it.

It was three stories tall, with a wraparound porch, a stained-glass window, a turret, wrought-iron balconies, and very beautifully decorated rooms—seven in all, not counting the porch, which had wicker furniture and fake plants and flowers on it.

There was a kitchen and a formal dining room on the lowest level. Then a master bedroom and living room on the second floor, and at the top, a children's room, a bathroom, and a playroom with a little crib in it.

All the rooms were wallpapered in tiny patterns, there were beautiful needlepoint and knitted rugs on all the floors, and embroidered curtains at every window. The living room furniture was upholstered and actually looked comfy, and the master bedroom had a bed with an upholstered headboard and a high canopy.

I heard my mom and my granny enter the room.

"It still works!" cried my mom.

"Actually, Jim got it working again," said my granny.

"It didn't need much," said my granddad modestly. "Just some wiring that had frayed, and a new battery system."

Listening to him talk, I began to formulate a

plan. "You're pretty handy, right, Granddad?" I said.

"Uh-oh!" He laughed. "What am I in for now?"

But I explained my project and what we needed, and he was thrilled to help. He had run a big construction company for many years, so building was his thing. I don't know why I didn't think of enlisting him earlier.

My granny scurried upstairs to get some paper, a pen, and a measuring tape and ruler. Meanwhile, my mom gave me a tour through the miniature house.

"Oh! I'd forgotten all about this! Look! Look at the tiny little plate of brownies, here in the kitchen! Gosh, we spent hours on this, my mom and I. And look at this! It's a real photo of me that my mom put in this itty-bitty frame. Wow. This really takes me back. I feel like I'm a kid again!"

I looked at my mom, smiling, her hair slipping out if its ponytail. She had a little smudge of dust on her chin, and her eyes were shining. For a second, I could picture her as a kid. I smiled at her. We would have been really good friends if we were the same age. I just know it.

"Hey, you need a plate of cupcakes for that kitchen!" I said, and we laughed.

✿

My granddad helped me with the measurements, and it took about an hour. He gave me all kinds of instructions, which I wrote down, for Matt on how to input things into the CAD program. (Actually, he offered to do it himself, because he has CAD too, but I wasn't about to pass up an offer from Matt!)

Along the way, my mom and my granny got bored and went upstairs for coffee. I asked them to pull together a few photos I could have for my time capsule, plus anything that showed how my mom used to dress, just out of curiosity.

When we'd finished with the measurements, I threw my arms around my granddad and thanked him. He had really saved the day.

"Oh, I remember all about school projects," he said, laughing and shaking his head. He winked at me. "Seems like they were always more work for the parents than anyone. Am I right?"

I laughed. "Usually, yes!"

"Now, if your friends have any trouble along the way with this, you'll call me up, okay? I can come and help you."

"Thanks. That's really nice of you."

We went upstairs to find my mom and my granny.

"Honey, anytime you want that dollhouse over at your place, I'd be happy to drive it in my pickup," said my granddad.

"Thanks! It's true. It wouldn't fit in our car," said my mom thoughtfully.

"Bring it home, Mom!" I cried. "I love it!"

She laughed. "I guess I should have tried again after that first time, with you and dollhouses. Maybe you were just too young and I was too eager to wait until you were the right age for it."

I shrugged. "Anyway, it *is* really cool. And you should have it nearby. Maybe you'll work on it again!"

"I'll talk to Dad about it. See if we can find a spot. Anyway, look at these horrible photos Granny found for you."

I sifted through the clutch of photos, laughing at the outfits my mom had on. The clothes were pretty ugly back in the eighties: plaid wool pants, stretchy leotardlike turtlenecks in rust colors. Ugh. Uncomfortable! Every time I giggled at one, I would hold it up for my mom to see, then she'd groan.

Then I came to a photo of her in a ballerina outfit—pink tights, pink leotard, ballet slippers, and her hair up in a tight bun.

"Hey! Was this for Halloween?" I asked.

My mom looked at it. "No, that was my ballerina stage."

"Stage?" Granny hooted. "That was a long stage! What was it, six years? Seven?"

"Wait, you were a dancer?" I asked my mom. I was shocked. "I mean, I knew you loved ballet, but I thought you loved watching it! I didn't know you *danced*! How come you never mentioned it?"

FYI, I am a great dancer. Not ballet, but I take modern dance after school a lot, and I am obsessed with ballroom dancing. My dad and I love to dance together. And I love the *Nutcracker Suite*, which my mom takes us to see in the city every year. You would think the fact she'd danced for so long would have come up. It seems like everything else has.

My mom waved her hand. "Oh, you know. I'm sure I mentioned it somewhere along the way. I didn't bring it up much, because I didn't want you girls to feel pressured to follow in my footsteps. You both tried ballet and weren't interested."

That was true. But still!

"She was a wonderful dancer," said my granny. "So graceful. So disciplined!"

I laughed. "That's not exactly a surprise!"

Granny looked thoughtful. "I think she liked

71

the structure, the rigidity. It gave her confidence. Right, honey?"

"Something like that," agreed my mom. "I really just liked to dance, though."

"Mom! You should do it again!" I cried. "Why did you stop?"

"Well, with ballet, you get to a point where you really have to commit to doing it full-time, and I didn't want to do that," she said. "Plus, a lot of the other dancers were mean." She winked at me. "It wasn't that healthy of a lifestyle, and very competitive."

"But you're competitive!" I said.

My mom laughed. "Thanks . . . I think! I guess I just channeled my competitiveness into school and then work. . . ."

"And Scrabble!" I reminded her. She never lets us beat her at that game, even when we were young.

"Right! And Scrabble!"

"Wow." I sat there, shaking my head in disbelief. I'd learned a lot about my mom today. "We've got to do this more often!" I declared.

My mom and my granny laughed.

"Anytime!" said my granny. "We love having you here!"

"We love being here," said my mom.

"Granny, can I take a couple of these and scan them for a project I'm working on? I'll return them to you," I said.

"Of course! What's this project, now?"

"A time capsule," I said. "My friends and I are making one, all about ourselves and a little bit about our moms, too." For some reason that second part was embarrassing. Like we were a fan club or something. I glanced sideways at my mom to see what she'd think.

"That's so sweet," she said, and I felt my shoulders sag in relief.

"You and your friends are just full of the best ideas!" said Granny.

"I know," I said with a grin. And I pocketed the photo of my mom as a ballerina, and the one of her all messy in the pear dress. They seemed to sum up everything anyone would need to know about her childhood.

On the way home in the car, I was kind of tired, so I mostly thought. I was surprised by some of the stuff I'd learned about my mom today. Well, some of it was unsurprising, like the perfectionism and whatever, but it was weird to learn new things about my very own mom after all these years. It made me wonder what else there is that I didn't know.

"Mom? What else don't I know about you?" I asked finally.

She laughed. "Oh, honey, I have no secrets. It's just ... Things come up as they come up, you know? It's not like it's easy to work things from my childhood into everyday conversation. They just come up as needed."

"Like Susan?" I said.

She laughed again. "Yes, like Susan."

"How did your dad die again?" I asked quietly. I can never remember this information. It's like I block it out.

"Meningitis. It was really sudden. They think he got it from a mosquito bite," she said.

"What's meningitis?"

"An infection that rapidly travels to your spine and then shuts down your body. Its main symptom is a really high, sudden fever."

Aha! No wonder my mom was always obsessing over whether we had fevers.

"Was it really hard for you guys when your dad died?" I asked. I didn't want to make her sad, but I felt so sorry for her after hearing what Granny said about her today.

She was quiet for a second, then she said, "You

74

know, it was really hard. My dad was a great guy. I felt vulnerable. All my friends had two parents, and I only had one. And I was scared that if something happened to Granny, then I would be without any parents at all. But it worked out okay. We were really lucky Granny and Jim found each other. He's been great for all of us, and he's a great granddad to you girls."

"He's really nice," I agreed. It was time to change the subject; enough of the sad stuff. "Mom. One more serious question."

"Mmm-hmm?"

"Why the heck did you dress like that in the eighties?"

CHAPTER 7

Friends and Enemies

When we got back late Saturday afternoon, I called Matt. I know, can you believe it? I just picked up the phone and then called him. Of course, my heart was fluttering the whole time, but I *did* need his help. Or I wanted his help, anyway!

We caught up for a minute and then I told him about the dollhouse. He was really psyched for me, saying it was a lucky break we'd be working off a model that was to size.

"Okay, so you're e-mailing me a photo of the house, and all the room dimensions, right?" he summarized.

"Yes. If you need any more info, I can either call my granddad or put you two in touch, or you can e-mail him directly."

"Cool," said Matt. "He's nice. I remember him from your holiday party."

"Yeah. I mean, yes!" I corrected myself, thinking of my mom.

"All right, so, I'll be in touch. Probably Monday, okay? I know you're in a rush."

"Thanks. There're lots of free cupcakes in this for you," I said.

"That's okay. Don't worry about it. I can use it in my portfolio." Matt is always trying to grow his digital graphic design business, so he takes on assignments from the Cupcake Club for posters and flyers, or this sort of thing. Then he uses them in his portfolio to show potential new clients what he can do. It is just another level that we connect on—as businesspeople, I mean.

"Great. Thanks!"

"Bye."

Next, I called Katie and explained my encounter with the Victorian dollhouse. She was thrilled, which made me feel really good. I e-mailed her the dollhouse photo, and we made a plan to visit the baking supply shop the next day. We'd work off the photo to find appropriate decorating supplies.

"This will be so much fun!" she squealed before we hung up.

77

After my calls, I felt much more in control of the project (even though it was really in Matt's hands now), as well as extremely lucky to have such generous and helpful friends. I spent the time until dinner researching Victorian-era houses online and working on my notecards for my presentation, and I got a really good chunk of work done. Not bad for a Saturday!

On Sunday morning I got up really early and basically finished the oral presentation component. I'd left a few spots where I'd have to see the finished model in order to insert a couple of facts, but I was in good shape. *Eat your heart out, Olivia Allen,* I thought.

I knocked off my other homework to clear the decks, and since I had a little time to spare, I started a spreadsheet to organize our time capsule. I had a sandwich, and then my mom took me to pick up Katie and then take us to the mall.

While she drove, Katie told my mom about what she'd collected for the time capsule so far.

"So, I have my tap dance shoes from when I was little, a recipe book with all my favorite recipes in it, and my stuffed bunny. The only bummer is that my favorite photo of me when I was little is with Callie," she said, looking at me sadly.

"Katie, that's totally okay!" I said brightly, trying to smooth over her still-hurt feelings from
her falling out with Callie. (Long story.) "I mean,
you can't just erase your past. It's what made you
who you are today. And she was a big part of
your life."

She shrugged. "But don't you think it's like I'm
sucking up to her if I put her in our time capsule?
And it's kind of disloyal to you guys."

"I don't mind," I said. And I was telling the
truth. "She's not that bad on her own. I think she
still likes you. Maybe you'll be friends again one
day." I wanted Katie to feel better.

"Do you think so?" asked Katie hopefully.

"Yeah," I said. "I mean, yes. Your moms are still
friends, anyway, right?"

Katie nodded and looked out the window.

I saw my mom glance at us in the rearview
mirror, and I met her eyes. She made a worried
face, like she felt bad for Katie but didn't want to
interfere.

"You know, Katie, when my mom was little,
there was a mean girl in her class named Susan . . . ,"
I began. And I met my mom's eyes again, and she
grinned.

❧

At the baking supply shop, Katie was excited and full of ideas. Since I am traditionally the business end and not the creative end of the Cupcake Club, my only goal was to stay within the budget my mom and I had set. But it was fun to watch Katie brainstorm. She can pick up a package of black candy wafers and say, "Roof tiles!" Or black licorice whips and say, "Wrought-iron railings!" It takes me a second, but then I get exactly what she's talking about and how perfect it will be.

We'd decided the base, or sidewalk, around the house would be red brick, so Katie suggested we paint matzo with a solution of red food coloring diluted in water to simulate brick. We could use frosting to glue them down. That was pure genius and not expensive, which made me very happy. I wrote "food coloring" and "matzo" on a list I'd started, because they'd be cheaper to get at the huge grocery store on Route 48. Into the basket went the candy wafers and the black licorice whips, though.

Katie said we'd use royal icing to pipe all the pretty white details around the outside of the doors and windows. The Cupcake Club has its own pastry bag and fittings, so I wrote "confectioners' sugar" on the grocery list—the main ingredient in making royal icing—and we kept looking. Katie picked out a package of something called "isomalt sticks," which looked like wax glow sticks and were clear in color. We'd melt them and then pour them out to harden into flat sheets, she said, and then trim them to use as window glass. I thought it sounded hard, but Katie assured me it would be one of those final touches that would take the house from normal to amazing. She told me to add vanilla wafer cookies to the grocery list, so we could use them to make the front stairs. (Katie said we're going to skip doing stairs inside because it's too much work and not that important. I was relieved. If it's too much for her, it would be insanely hard for me!)

It didn't take us long to find everything we needed. Mom would take us to the grocery store next.

We were chatting happily as we spun out of the store and right into Callie and Olivia. Ugh. Why do we always seem to be at the mall at the same time as those girls? I'd been having so much fun, I hadn't given Olivia any thought in almost an hour. My palms were instantly sweaty, like I was gearing up for a confrontation, though I knew I'd avoid talking with her at any expense.

"Hey," said Callie cautiously. We all think she

still likes Katie but thinks she can't be seen being friends with her because it will affect her status in life or something. Callie didn't actually stop moving her feet, but she kind of slowed down and turned back to face us, like she might stop.

"Oh, hey," said Katie casually.

I could see Katie struggling with whether to stop and chat or keep walking. I wanted to keep walking—and not because of Callie!

Olivia gave me a dirty look and flounced her hair, but at least she didn't make some snarky comment. She didn't even break her stride.

We kept walking, and the encounter was over.

A little ways down the hall, we got on the escalator, and I finally breathed a sigh of relief. "Awk-ward!" I singsonged, but Katie was quiet.

"Katie?" I asked.

She turned reluctantly toward me, and her eyes had tears welling up in them. "Oh, Katie!" I cried, and then I tried to give her a hug. Hugging on escalators is not a good idea, by the way, and I recommend you never try it. But at least our nearly crashing to our deaths got Katie giggling, and her unshed tears only leaked a little.

"Sorry." She sniffled, but the crisis had passed. "I just couldn't believe that we'd just been talking about her, and then there she was, with her new life!"

"I know," I agreed quietly.

"And then . . . I had nothing to say to her! Nothing! And she used to be my best friend!" Katie's lip quivered.

"Well, I bet she would never have asked you to do a whole class project of hers, now would she?" I joked. "And she never would have made you march in a parade in costume, so she could be with her crush, huh? Would she? Now what kind of a friend is that?" These were all things Katie did for me.

Katie got giggling again.

"Anyway, how about me? I feel like I'm going to throw up whenever I see Olivia. I'm surprised she didn't figure out a way to insult me as she strolled on by! Like, maybe she could have said, 'Hey, Alexis, looks like you're having a hard time walking with that bag full of fattening supplies!'"

Katie grew serious. "Is she still doing that?"

"Totally," I said. My stomach clenched, dreading seeing her in school.

"It's funny she didn't do it just now, when there were other people around."

"I know. She's a sneak attacker," I said. Now I felt miserable. We had almost reached my mom's car. "And the worst part is, my mom thinks I need to apologize to her!"

"What?" Katie was shocked, but I couldn't finish the story now.

"I'll tell you at the grocery store," I whispered. "Hi, Mom!" I called in a fake-cheery voice, getting into the car. I gave Katie a serious look, and she nodded; we would not be discussing any of this with my mom.

At the grocery store we filled the cart with the items from the list I'd made, plus the gingerbread ingredients we'd need. Katie also threw in some waxed paper and a couple of other supplies that would come in handy.

As we walked, we discussed what I should do about Olivia. Katie understood my mom's point about apologizing, but she knows Olivia as well as I do. She knows that apologizing might only set me up as a permanent victim in Olivia's eyes.

"That girl does *not* need a new punching bag," Katie said seriously.

She had a point.

"But I need to apologize. It wasn't nice of me to say that. But it also doesn't justify the way she's been treating me. So after I apologize, then I want to follow it up with something strong, you know?"

"Yes, and at the same time. Like, you can't let the apology hang out there and then later do something strong, because she'll be gathering her strength, thinking she's beaten you after the apology. And then you'll never beat her. Let's think of a plan."

"Okay."

I loved that Katie was always helping me. She is a good friend, and I can't in a million years think of why Callie would have thrown her over for that mean and snobby group of girls. It really meant that something was wrong with Callie. Anyway, we didn't come up with a plan right then, but Katie promised to keep thinking about it, and obviously, I would too.

We finished our shopping and then checked out. The purchase was expensive, and I was not psyched. I like to make money, not spend it. Let me correct that. I don't mind laying out cash if I know I'll make some back on the outlay, but I hate spending money like this, knowing it will go to nothing. I tried explaining this to Katie.

"But you'll get a good grade!" she protested. "And you love good grades!"

"I know, but it's like buying a grade."

"Lots of kids buy grades. I mean, that's what tutoring is, isn't it?"

"Maybe . . ." (That made me stop and think. Maybe tutoring would be a good business to get into one day. Good hours, working with kids, doing stuff you already know how to do, being your own boss . . .)

"Earth to Alexis!" said Katie, and we laughed.

My mom took us for ice cream after the shopping, and we had a lot of fun.

We didn't run into anyone we knew, and that was just fine by me.

That night, as I lay in my bed in the dark, I thought about Olivia and why she makes me feel so bad. I think it's because she knows how to hit me where it hurts by accusing me of nerdiness and some kind of pigginess, as if all I do is think about food or sweets or homework. In general, I am having a great time living my life. I love school, I like working hard and getting good grades. I like running a business and making money, and I love my friends and family (except Dylan—not all the time, anyway). But I do sometimes wonder if I'm doing it all wrong. Like, maybe I should be out trying to run with the cool pack or not caring so much about doing well, but instead relaxing more and just hanging out. Maybe I'm trying too hard to be a little adult. Maybe I *am* a nerd.

Am I?

Do I care?

"Yes, a little bit" is the answer to both, but I'm not going to do anything about it. Like I said, I'm mostly happy in my life. Except whenever I see Olivia.

I rolled over, thinking with dread about what attack she would come up with tomorrow and whether it would be quiet and mean or public and humiliating. I thought about apologizing, but also what I could then do or say to gain back my power from her.

Sighing deeply, I tried to come to terms with the idea that it wouldn't be something I could plan ahead for; it would just have to happen naturally. In the wild.

CHAPTER 8

Duck!

I met Matt at school Monday morning before classes started. He was dropping off the plans so Katie and I could review them during lunch. It was a treat and a good omen. After all, if your week starts with a great interaction with your crush, you're starting from a position of strength. At least that's how I chose to see it (rather than that things could only go downhill from there).

He had the outer dimensions of the house plans ready to go and just had to put in the floor dimensions for the upper two stories. He said he'd have it for me by five o'clock today if I wanted to stop by after school. I wanted to hug him in gratitude, but I didn't have the nerve, so I just thanked him profusely.

"It was fun," he said. "The notes from you and your granddad were good. Very detailed, but I'd expect nothing less." He grinned.

"Thanks!" I said, choosing not to see this as a sign that he considered me a detail-obsessed nerd. I wished Olivia and her little flock would walk by me right now so they could see me laughing it up with Matt Taylor, supercutie! But of course they didn't. It did give me an idea, though.

I took a deep breath and screwed up my courage. "Hey, maybe when it's done, you can help me carry it to school on the presentation day? I think it's going to be a little heavy."

"Sure, just let me know when," he said, really easily, just like that.

Yessss! I thought. *Eat your heart out, Olivia Allen!* But all I said was, "Okay, thanks! See you later!"

After Matt left, I walked slowly to homeroom, happily daydreaming about when he and I get married and how we'd run a big successful corporation of our own and have a couple of children who are really smart and really good dancers . . .

After homeroom I heard someone behind me say, "I hope you got your fill at the baking store this weekend. I thought that place was just for old grandmas."

I didn't even need to turn around to see who it was. *Quack!* I reminded myself. *Quack! Quack!* But it wasn't working. I pretended I didn't hear her, but inside I was panicking.

Olivia continued, "Hey! I heard there's a new math store opening up. They're selling all the types of things that you love, like calculators and rulers and—"

"Quack!" I blurted, turning around to face her. She froze.

"Quack! Quack! Quackquackquack!!!" I yelled.

I knew I had just sealed my fate as a nerd for life, but I was so angry, I had totally lost control. The small, careful part of my brain that was still working knew that quacking was better than yelling bad words at Olivia in the middle of school, but even if it kept me out of trouble, it would mean certain social death.

People around us were staring, and I knew it must've made a strange picture, her cringing and me towering over her, quacking loudly and red faced. I was shaking, though, and I didn't care right now what anyone else thought. I was just trying hard not to smack her.

Finally, she snapped to and said, "What-*ever*, weirdo!" and walked on, her head held high.

I stayed put, to give myself time to calm down and to let her get a head start away from me. A couple of kids were giving me odd looks, and I was embarrassed. I took a deep breath and then went to the girls' bathroom, where I took some sips of cold water and splashed my face. I was exhausted after my outburst, and wished I could just go to the nurse and ask to go home. Instead, because I am not a quitter, I trudged off to math, where I knew my enemy awaited me.

In class, Olivia and I avoided eye contact, and when the bell rang, she slipped out of her seat, racing for the door while I held back. At least she wasn't trying to continue the fight. I wouldn't have had the strength to face her again. I made my way to gym and the safety of my friends.

Of course, by the time I'd reached them, they'd already heard about the incident from other people. I was mortified the story had spread so quickly. I put my head in my hands and rocked it from side to side.

"Alexis! Stop doing that! Right now!" Mia commanded in a serious voice as she quickly scanned the gym.

I lifted my head. "What? Why?"

"Because you're a hero, but you're acting like a

loser!" she said, looking sharply back at me.

"What?" I was confused. I was a nerd, and I knew it.

Mia sighed in exasperation. "Kids are talking about how you stood up to Olivia Allen in the hall and won. If you act like you lost, the story will start to change. Get it?"

"Sort of," I said.

"Just act proud," said Emma.

"Really?" This was weird, because I did not feel proud at all.

"Yes." Emma nodded. "Trust us."

Our gym teacher, Mrs. Chen, kept us too busy to talk during class so I couldn't tell them what happened in detail. Finally at lunch we all got to sit down and talk.

"Now, what happened?" Katie asked, and I told them the whole story, including how Mom always told me to let things roll off my back.

Actually, the timing was perfect, because right as they were roaring with laughter, picturing me having a duck meltdown in the hall, Olivia walked into the lunchroom. She looked directly at me and my table of friends, laughing our heads off, and she turned on her heel and left.

"You just won," said Katie, who'd been watching the door. "Did you see that?"

I nodded, but I didn't feel good about it. "It's not over."

"I think you're wrong," said Katie, shrugging.

"We'll see," I said.

We planned a meeting for later that day at Emma's and then, at my insistence, talked about other stuff for the rest of lunch. But deep down inside I let myself relax a tiny bit. Maybe I *hadn't* committed sudden social death.

"Okay, a few things on the agenda today . . . ," I began at Emma's kitchen table that afternoon.

"Quack!" said Katie, and she giggled.

"Quack, quack!" said Mia.

"All right, enough!" I cried.

"Sorry," said Mia with a smile.

I cleared my throat. "On the agenda—"

"Quack!" Emma peeped in a tiny voice.

"Stop!" I hollered, but I had to giggle.

"Quack! Quack! Quack!" They all were doing it at the same time.

I put down my ledger, where I keep track of everything. "Okay, you know what? Fine. Just get it out of your system, okay? We have a business to run here, and we need to discuss some other important items, so when you are ready to act like mature people and not like idiots . . ."

They quacked and laughed for another minute, and then we began for real.

"We have the shower this weekend, which we'll need to bake for on Friday, along with Mona's minis. We also have my mom's birthday, and I had a great idea. Since she's turning forty-four, we'll make forty-four cupcakes, eleven of each kind of the following: pear, something pink and ballerina-ish, the strawberry shortcake she requested, plus the bacon ones for my dad. It will be a little cupcake buffet. Okay?"

Everyone nodded.

"No duck cupcakes?" asked Mia with a smile.

"No," I said sharply. "Next, we have the time capsule project. I made a few notes on this." I pulled out some spreadsheets and then distributed them. "As you can see, there's a checklist and then a Q&A section. Everyone needs to fill in their answers to the questions, and everyone should provide one of each of the items on the checklist. Just let me know what you think needs to be added or deleted. It's only a starting point."

Emma was scanning the list. "This is going to

have to be a really big capsule!" she said.

"I know," I agreed. "I was almost thinking instead of putting the actual items in, we should just take a picture of them . . ."

"And we can put a printout of the pictures and a flash drive with everything on it!" finished Mia.

"Exactly," I said, grinning.

"Great idea! Then the capsule can be really small!" said Katie.

"And we don't have to part with the things we love," added Emma.

"Right. So is there anything I should add or remove?"

Everyone was quiet while they read their sheet. Then Katie said quietly, "The part about sworn enemies . . . Do you think we need that?"

I bit my lip. "I wasn't sure, but I thought it would maybe give us a chance to share what we've learned with future generations, like how to deal with bullies and mean girls."

"By quacking?" teased Emma.

"Very funny," I said. "Not."

Mia was thoughtful. "Maybe it should be a more open-ended question. Like, who was the meanest person you ever dealt with and how did you handle it?"

"An essay question?" I cried in dismay.

But the others thought it was a really good idea.

"I know who I'm writing about!" said Katie. (We all did.)

"Syd the Kid, à la Sydney Whitman, will be mine!" declared Emma. "Not that I can take credit for the Whitmans moving to California, but still, that solved it."

"Who's moving to California?" asked Matt as he ambled into the Taylors' kitchen from outside.

My heart skipped a beat. He was wearing a light blue hoodie that made his eyes look electric, and his hair was all wind-tousled and messy. So cute. Sigh!

"Hey, Alexis, I'm just going to run up and finish the plans. I'll be right down with the printouts," he said.

"Great. Thanks."

"So tomorrow is our baking day?" said Katie. "For the project?"

"Yup. Maybe at my house?"

Katie agreed, and Emma and Mia wanted to come too.

"You guys must have lots of other stuff to do. I think Katie and I can handle it. I feel bad taking up your time with my project."

But they insisted.

"Look, like Katie said, this could be a whole new line of revenue for us!" Mia pointed out.

"We wouldn't miss it," said Emma firmly.

That night I pulled my dad aside and told him about the plans for the cupcakes. I also told him about a few ideas I had for presents for my mom, including a spot for her dollhouse and having my granddad deliver it before the weekend.

My dad loved all my ideas and said I was very thoughtful, which, of course, I liked to hear. I don't know if he would have said it if he knew I'd quacked at someone at school today.

When my mom came to tuck me in, I couldn't bear telling her about what had happened with Olivia today. I knew she'd chastise me for being mean and also for not having apologized yet, and I didn't want her to be disappointed in me. But I could tell she knew I was holding something back by the way she kept asking questions but nothing directly.

In the end, she gave me a kiss and said she's always available for discussions.

Phew.

CHAPTER 9

Rallying

$\mathcal{T}$he day of reckoning had arrived. On Tuesday afternoon, it was time to bake the gingerbread and to begin the house. I felt like I was on one of those cooking challenge shows, with all the crazy ingredients assembled before me. Licorice whips, molasses, ginger, sprinkles, eggs, flour, cookies; plus rulers and knives and paper . . . It was wild.

But first, the gingerbread.

Katie and I made a triple batch in my mom's huge KitchenAid mixer. Mia and Emma actually sat at the kitchen table and did homework while we did that, because it was the "boring part."

When it was time to roll out the dough, and cut and score it, they came and helped hold the templates—which I'd cut out last night—in place over the dough, and offered opinions on how things should be laid out on the pans. This was deemed the "hard part." I only hoped it wouldn't get much harder than this. Compared to gingerbread architecture, baking cupcakes is a sweet walk in the park.

While we worked, we discussed the spreadsheets for the time capsule and made a plan to shoot the photos of our items on Saturday at my house, after my mom's birthday party.

Katie slid the trays into the oven to bake. We'd have to do about six rounds of baking before all the gingerbread was done. It smelled good, but it was not that appetizing looking, all shiny and brown. Katie laid out the next slabs of dough on waxed paper and tweaked them a little. I felt useless, watching her work.

"Any sightings today?" asked Mia. "I didn't see her in homeroom this morning."

I knew who she meant. "No," I said.

"She was absent," said Emma, not looking up from her notebook.

"What?" I was shocked. "How do you know?"

Emma looked up. "She's in my science class. Some kid told the teacher."

"I wonder if she was sick . . . ," I said.

"Or just scared!" cackled Mia.

"Don't even joke. I don't want to be a mean girl. You know that. After all, I'd be doing to her just what she's been doing to me, and look how bad it made me feel."

We were all quiet for a minute.

"Well, let's see if she has the sniffles tomorrow," said Katie, quietly cutting dough on the counter.

For whatever reason that got us giggling, and any discussion of Olivia was finally put aside. I did feel guilty, though, and I had been all day. I'd actually been looking for her at lunch, planning to apologize and just get the whole thing over with, but, as usual, when I want to see her, she's nowhere to be found.

The time passed slowly, and batches of dough went in and came out. Katie trimmed them carefully after they came out, to get rid of the puffiness they get from baking, then she laid them out on racks to cool. I was amazed by how she knew to do all this stuff and finally had to ask.

"Well, my grandmother likes to bake, and we bake a lot together. Every Christmas we make a simple gingerbread house. And my mom is really good with her hands, you know, because she's a dentist. Obviously, I kind of inherited that. The good with the hands part, not the dentist part. And then I went to that cooking camp and learned some stuff. And, you know, I watch cooking shows and go online to read about baking all the time. It's just . . . a lot of the skills transfer from project to project pretty easily."

"Cool," I said, thinking it was the same with my business skills.

Just then the doorbell rang, and it was the UPS guy. He handed me a package addressed to me, and I signed for it, wondering what it could be. Then I looked at the return address.

"It's from my grandma! She found the pear dress!" I said, shaking the box and hearing something soft shift around inside. "I've got to run upstairs and hide this," I said. And it was lucky I had, because when I came back down, my mom had arrived home from work and was chatting with my friends in the kitchen.

"Girls, I've got some bad news," she said, but she was smiling. "I've got to make dinner, so we're going to need to close the bake shop for the night."

"But, Mom!" I protested. "We're right in the middle of it!"

"I'm sorry, but I'm sure I speak for all moms everywhere when I say, it's time for dinner, and it's time for people to be doing their own homework at their own desks. Though I very much appreciate your friends helping you," she said with a smile. "I'm going to run up and change while you clear this up."

"Aargh!" I made an annoyed noise. "We're almost done!" I said, but she didn't even turn around.

"Here, let me just trim this one, and you take that one . . . ," Katie said, switching the trays around, and then—*crash!* Just as I was taking it from her hands, a tray fell to the floor, and the large slab of gingerbread split into three pieces. It was totally my fault, although Katie began yelling "I'm so sorry!" at the top of her lungs.

"No!" I cried. "We don't have time for error!" I dropped to my knees and lifted the tray back up. Biting my lip, I surveyed the damage. The others gathered around. "It's totally not your fault, Katie," I said.

"You can just make another one tomorrow, can't you?" asked Emma.

"No! I need to be building tomorrow. Because Thursday is decorating, and it's due Friday."

"I bet we can glue it back together with frosting," said Katie. She looked at her watch. "You know what, I do have to get home because I totally spaced that we have the math rally on Thursday, and unlike some people, it is *not* my best subject. I need to study."

"Okay. I totally understand. Thanks, you guys. Thank you all so much for helping me."

"It was fun!" said Katie, shrugging on her jacket.

Everyone cleaned up a little, but I shooed them out and did the rest myself. This way, I figured, if any more gingerbread broke, I'd only have myself to blame. I was so grateful to them for helping me, and I felt terrible that it was basically a three-night project. I knew I'd taken on too much—cheered along by Katie's enthusiasm and willingness to help—but now I'd have to see it through. However, I didn't foresee what would happen next.

Late that night, I was just about to shut down my computer when I spotted an IM from Katie. It said:

OMG Alexis I am so so so so sorry, but my mom quizzed me on my math, and I did so badly, she said I have to come straight home from school tomorrow and study. She'll quiz me when she gets home, and if I do okay, I can come help you, but otherwise I have to stay home. I'm so sorry! Call me if you get this before 9:30.

I looked at my watch: 10:20.

I sat heavily on the edge of my bed. What was I going to do?

This was something that quacking would not help.

I was still sitting there ten minutes later, lost in thoughts of possibilities, when my mom came in to say good night.

"My goodness! You're not even in bed yet and it's ten thirty!"

I looked up, startled.

"What's wrong?" she said, sitting down on my spare bed to face me.

"I have to build this gingerbread house all by myself tomorrow, and I have no idea what I'm doing."

"What happened?" she asked, and I explained.

"Listen, sweetheart, do you absolutely have to do this immense and difficult project? Can't we just quit while we're ahead and help you with a pretty costume?"

"No!" I said forcefully. This presentation was going to kick butt. It had to.

"Okay, that's pretty definite," said my mom.

Then the two of us sat there for a minute, thinking.

Finally, my mom said, "What we need is someone who isn't at work, doesn't have homework, and knows how to build."

And at the exact same minute our heads snapped up, and we looked at each other. "Granddad!"

She jumped up from the bed. "I'm going to call him now!" she said.

"At ten forty?" I cried as she fled out of my room.

"They always stay up for the eleven o'clock news. Anyway, this is an e-mer-gen-cy!" she trilled as she ran down the stairs.

I sat on my bed, too nervous to chase her and listen in. I just focused all my energy on hoping Granddad would be free and able to come. I crossed every finger and toe and squeezed my eyes tight. Finally, I couldn't take it anymore. I left my room and tiptoed to the top of the stairs, where I could just make out my mom's end of the conversation.

"Yes, she gets out at three. That would be perfect. Thank you so much. Oh my gosh, we can't tell you how much we appreciate this. Thank you!"

I pumped my fist in the air. Victory!

❀

The next morning at school, I told my friends how my granddad was coming and that they could have the afternoon off. I was actually relieved, because it just didn't feel right for them to spend so much time on my project. Katie insisted she'd come by after she was done, but I asked her to save the trip until Thursday, when I'd really need her.

I walked quickly to math, knowing who would be there and on my team for the math rally practice too. I just wanted to get it over with, though. I hated Mr. Donnelly for a minute right then, for putting Olivia and me together. It was such a total downer. But the sooner it was finished, the better.

In the classroom, he'd already moved the chairs around into little clusters. But there wasn't anyone there yet. I sat in my seat, and guess who walked in next?

She and I looked at each other, caught and frozen, like deer in headlights. I opened my mouth to say something, but Mr. Donnelly came bustling in with a cheery hello. The moment had passed, and the room quickly filled.

Our group was good, and I hated to admit it, but Olivia was one of the best (along with yours truly, of course). She didn't say one mean thing to me for almost the entire class, either. Actually, she didn't say anything to me. She just acted like I wasn't there. She did say one meanish thing to George Martinez when he missed a question, but that was all. I started to wonder if my friends were right. Maybe I *had* won. It was a weird, new feeling—kind of powerful—and I'm embarrassed to admit to myself that I kind of like it.

But then I got a really hard question I knew the answer to, and in my excitement, I jumped up, and my chair knocked back and tipped over. Everyone laughed, including Mr. Donnelly and finally, me. It was funny, I realized. When I'd successfully answered the question and sat back down, Olivia leaned over, so everyone could hear, and said, "Very exciting. Kind of like a bake-off, right, Alexis?"

So I turned to look her right in the eye and said, "Meet me after class." Just like that!

OMG. After I said it, my whole body flooded with a cold feeling, then a hot feeling. My knees wobbled, and I didn't look around to see who'd heard me. I just willed myself not to blush. What the heck was I going to say to Olivia Allen after class? I did not know. All I knew was that this had gone on long enough and it was totally distracting me.

The remaining fifteen minutes of class flew by,

of course, and when the bell rang, I rose, packed my things, and waited for Olivia outside the door. It took her so long, I had to look back in to see if she slipped by without me seeing her (which really would have been impossible), but she was still there, slowly loading her bag.

Finally, finally, just when I thought I couldn't take it anymore, she came through the door and into the hall.

She stopped and then looked at me with a challenging tilt to her chin. "So?" she asked. "What do you want?"

I took a deep breath and just plunged in.

"To apologize. I may have said something rude about you, and I'm sure you heard about it. I wanted to apologize and to say that it wasn't nice and probably wasn't true."

Olivia just stared at me. A moment went by, and then she said, "It isn't true. I happen to be a really good skier. We used to go all the time."

So Maggie was right! Olivia *had* been holding this grudge all this time. Wow.

"Well, I am sorry for being mean. I regret hurting your feelings. And now I'd like you to apologize as well." I can't believe my nerve!

"For what?" Olivia asked, narrowing her eyes.

"For treating me terribly. For embarrassing me on purpose. For teasing me, mocking me, and humiliating me. What I said was wrong, but your punishment has been unbearable, and it needs to stop."

Olivia blinked.

"Well . . . ," she started. "Thanks. Thanks for apologizing. I didn't know why you said that, and I thought it was really mean."

"It was," I said. But I had to hold my ground. I wanted Olivia to apologize too. I took another deep breath. "But probably not mean enough that you had to torture me for the past few weeks. You were really mean back, and it's a terrible way to treat another person. Also, I'm not sure why you are so fascinated by me that you are always watching me. I guess I'm flattered."

Olivia looked around. None of her BFFs were around, and it was just Olivia and me. Was Olivia nervous? Embarrassed? I couldn't tell. "I don't watch you all the time," she finally said.

"Well, you seem to pay attention to a lot of things I do. I guess I'm just really interesting to watch."

Olivia tossed her hair. "It's not personal, Alexis."

"Oh, but it is," I said. "Especially when you

embarrass me. I mean, look how upset you got when I made fun of you for possibly not being a good skier. And that was only once!"

Olivia flinched. "I guess I'm sorry too, then."

We stared at each other for a moment longer, then I put out my hand. She looked down at it kind of scornfully, but then she took it, and we shook hands.

And then she walked away.

Meanwhile, I was about to faint. I fell back against a locker and just rested there to regain my strength before moving on. Could this be the end of it? It felt like a dream. I hoped it wasn't.

CHAPTER 10

The Finishing Touches

At lunch—I couldn't believe it—but I didn't run and find my friends to gloat. I grabbed a tray, loaded it up, and ate lunch alone in the math lab. I felt like a traitor and a chicken, but somehow, I couldn't face them and then not tell them what happened, but I also didn't want to sit at lunch and go through a huge I-said–she-said thing. Weirdly, it seemed disloyal to Olivia. What happened after math was private. I needed a little while to think of a way to sum it up to my friends that was truthful but vague.

After school I flew home on my bike to find my granddad's pickup in the driveway. He had some big thing under a tarp in the bed of the truck, and I hoped it wasn't a power tool we needed for the gingerbread house!

"Yahoo!" I yelled, and raced into the house.

"Hi, honey!" he called out upon seeing me.

I ran to him and gave him a huge squeeze, then I pulled away and beamed at him.

"Thank you!" I cried.

He hugged me again and said, "Glad to be of service, ma'am. Let's see what you've got."

So I walked him through the plans and showed him the gingerbread slabs, the outlines Matt had done, and explained what we needed to do. He seemed unruffled by all of it, but I guess when you've spent fifty years building big houses, a little gingerbread one doesn't seem so hard.

"Okay, so first, I'll lay out the board for the base, and then I'll make the royal icing," I said.

"Actually, first, I want you to help me to get your mom's present out of the truck," he said.

"Okay, what is it?"

"The dollhouse! Your dad called this morning and asked me to bring it."

I clapped my hands. "Yay! Do you think we need to hide it?"

"I think so."

I scurried to open the doors to the basement, and we carefully carried the dollhouse down there, setting it on my dad's workbench.

"He's going to make a stand for it and put it in the sunroom, from what I understand," said my granddad, winking at me. My dad's not that handy, but he always tries to make things, and Granddad always comes and fixes them. Kind of like me with the gingerbread house, I guess!

"We're really keeping you busy, Granddad!" I giggled.

When we finished with the dollhouse, we went back upstairs, brought in my granddad's overnight bag (he'd sleep over here tonight, because it would probably be late when we finished), and then we began.

I made the icing while he surveyed the pieces and got things lined up in the order in which we'd build them.

"We should build the three floors separately and then give them as long as possible to dry and set. Then we can construct the whole house," he said after a minute. "Because you won't have the time to let this dry in stages overnight. We might need to use some supports in the end—which is tricky— but we'll see how it goes."

Meanwhile, the icing was kind of runny. I lifted the spoon and poured some out. "This doesn't look right," I said with a frown.

He came over and looked into the bowl. "Add more sugar. Thicken it up," he suggested.

"You think?"

He laughed. "That's what you do with cement if it's too runny. Just add more powder!"

"Okay!" Now I was laughing too. But it worked!

The first thing we did was repair the broken wall. We could assemble that section last, to give it time to stabilize. My granddad said if it didn't work, we could add some stabilizers. He'd brought something called dowels, among other things, that we could set in with frosting to hold things in place. I hoped it didn't come to that.

Dylan came home after a while, then my mom, and finally my dad. My dad and granddad exchanged a nod and a wink when my mom wasn't looking, and my granddad gestured down, as if to say, *It's in the basement.* Meaning the dollhouse, of course.

The gingerbread house didn't look like much at that stage, and it was still pretty portable, so my mom had us move the assembly from the counter to the kitchen table; we'd eat in the dining room since my granddad was here.

As we picked up the various sections, a few walls began to wobble.

"Oh no!"

My mom jumped over to steady them, and we inched to the table.

"Phew!" I said, setting it down.

"You couldn't have made a costume?" my mom teased.

My granddad and I looked at each other, and smiled.

"Nah. Too easy," he said.

"Costumes are for wimps!" I added.

The timing worked out well. We ate dinner while the glued sections dried, then we went back to work. It was nearly nine o'clock when we set the sections on top of one another. However, things started to wobble almost immediately, and my granddad rushed to lift the second story off the first.

"Supports," he said grimly. "We're gonna need 'em after all."

I'm a little ashamed to tell you the next part of this story, but here's the truth of what happened: I went to bed, and my parents and my granddad stayed up till midnight finishing the gingerbread house. It's horrible but true. In business, it's called "outsourcing," which means having someone else do the work when you can't. Of course, you would usually pay those people, and I'm not about to pay my relatives, so the comparison ends there. The bottom line is, I bit off more than I could chew, and all to show off to an enemy. What a sorry reason for a project.

However, when I woke up the next morning, it felt like Christmas. I ran downstairs, and there it was, in the middle of the kitchen table: the finished gingerbread house, identical (in shape, anyway) to my mom's dollhouse.

"Oh!" I said, clapping my hands.

I heard someone behind me, and turned.

"Turned out pretty great, didn't it?" said my granddad, sipping his coffee.

"It's awesome. Thank you *so* much!" I gave him a big hug.

"Only one problem," he said.

"What?"

"How're you going to fit this thing in your car?"

It wasn't long before we realized that the only solution would be for my granddad to come back with his tarp and his truck and everything again tomorrow to transport the house to school. I don't know how I'll ever thank this man enough. All I know is, I'm glad I lined up Matt to help when we got there!

❧

That afternoon, my house was a festival of sugar. Katie, Mia, Emma, and I were like whirling dervishes getting this house finished. We had four little workstations, and we were like elves—busy, busy!

Katie trimmed and set the wrought-iron railings along the porch and roof with frosting and black licorice whips. That was the hardest part, if you ask me.

I shingled the roof with black candy wafers.

Mia piped white decorative trim around the windows as shutters and window frames. And Emma created the windows (the second hardest thing).

After about an hour, it was really looking good. After two hours, it was incredible. Katie wanted to keep going, but I had to put on my CEO hat and say enough was enough. We could work on this thing forever, but after a certain point it wasn't worth it. The result was already spectacular, and we didn't need to go on; it just wouldn't be an efficient use of our time.

Mia took out her phone and snapped dozens of photos for our website. We even e-mailed a couple to Matt, so he could see how well it turned out, and some to my grandparents, since they were in on it from the beginning. And, of course, we'd print out a photo for our time capsule.

We cleaned up, and then I sent my friends home with huge hugs and profuse thank-yous. We had a big day again tomorrow, so a break would do us all good. Plus, everyone had homework, and I had to put in the last finishing touches to my oral report.

After they left, I sat for a minute in the kitchen, admiring our work. It was really beautiful. It was funny how you felt like you could just keep working on something—adding this or that cute thing, improving what you'd already done, thinking up a clever new detail. It made me understand how my mom must've felt working on her real dollhouse. It could be an endless project if you wanted it to be.

When my family got home, they were totally wowed by the gingerbread house. Inside, I was bursting with pride, but I played it cool. The truth was, I still couldn't wait to see Olivia's face tomorrow when I brought it in. I knew I shouldn't care, but I did.

That night, I went up to my room and took one last look at my time capsule spreadsheet. I'd filled in pretty much everything, proudly inking in my mother's childhood hobbies (ballet dancing, doll-houses) and my own (math, business), as well as my goals for the future (the aforementioned marrying of Matt Taylor and running a large company). But the part I'd left blank, the part about enemies, I was finally ready to fill in.

I didn't want to name names, because things can change, and it just seemed so negative. Instead I gave a long answer.

Sometimes people will try your patience or do things that you think are pretty mean. But there's always a solution, even if it's not an easy one. You just need to remember all the good things you have going on in your life and let the not-so-good stuff roll off your back. Just act like a duck. Quack and let it roll off your back. My mom taught me that.

I lined up most of the items I'd be photographing for the capsule: my business ledger; the pretty pink dress I wore to Dylan's sweet sixteen when Matt asked me to dance; a DVD of the first season of *Celebrity Ballroom*; a tag from my favorite store, Big Blue; and a photo of me in my homecoming parade costume, where I dressed up as a Greek goddess and went with Matt. I was pretty happy with the collection. At the last minute I added an eraser shaped like a cupcake, and a calculator, because why not?

Then I sat back, relaxed, and let myself daydream for a moment about being Mrs. Matt Taylor. I hoped our children would have his blond hair. Our babies would be smart *and* beautiful! It was the best daydream ever.

CHAPTER 11

Success!

My granddad arrived early Friday morning; he was there before I even got up. After a hasty breakfast, we carefully loaded the gingerbread house onto the bed of his truck, where he secured it with all sorts of padding and blankets and bungee cords and stuff. I couldn't look, but I trusted him. He'd also brought a little folding trolley that we could use to wheel the house into school.

We swung by the Taylors', and Matt came out to hop in for the ride. His parents and Emma and his little brother, Jake, came out too, to see the creation in the back of the truck. Everyone oohed and aahed over it, and I was really proud.

At school, Katie met us at the door. She had also come early. I am not that sentimental, but I had to say I was feeling a little teary and grateful for all these wonderful people who were helping me. I was pretty lucky I had them, or I would never have pulled it off. It reminded me of what my mom had said when we discussed Olivia. ("You are great the way you are. You have wonderful friends, a family who loves you, and one big, bad Olivia shouldn't get in the way of any of that. You need to act like a duck.") Quack!

I had made prearrangements to hide the gingerbread house in the teachers' lounge, so that it would be a surprise for our class, so that was where we wheeled it. The teachers who were there kind of freaked out at how cool it was, including Mr. Donnelly, which was nice since he's my favorite.

"Alexis! I had no idea you had this much artistic talent!" he said.

"Well, I had lots of help," I admitted, smiling at my granddad, Katie, and Matt.

We left the table, and Matt said he'd meet me back there during his study hall period to wheel the house in with me. I hugged my granddad good-bye and promised to call to let him know how it went. I hugged Katie too, and she left a little tub of frosting and a mini-spatula on the trolley, in case I needed it later.

I could barely sit still through homeroom, and I literally ran to the faculty lounge when it was time to pick up the trolley. Matt was already there, waiting for me. He must've run, too, which made me even more grateful.

"Ready?" he asked, with his adorable dimples and grin.

"Ready!" I said, and off we went through the halls.

Everyone we passed stopped in their tracks to look at the house. It was really spectacular. Plus, you don't usually see that much candy wheeling through school every day. I couldn't wait to see Olivia's face. Even though we'd made peace, this would be the icing on the cake!

Slowly, slowly we made our way down the hall. There was almost no one left by the time we reached our destination. Into Mrs. Carr's classroom we went, and everyone was already there, seated. For a moment, there was dead silence, then Sara Rex started to clap, and everyone joined in. Olivia (dressed as a fancy Victorian lady, in a high-waisted shirt and a long-sleeved, high-necked blouse) had a look of wonder on her face, shaking her head in disbelief, even as she clapped. I met her eye and smiled a small smile, and she smiled back. Pretty soon the whole class was cheering, and I was grinning, and finally, Mrs. Carr had to quiet everyone down.

Matt ducked out with a wave, and Mrs. Carr said, "Alexis, I think you should go first."

I put down my bag, got out my notecards, and began talking about home life in Victorian England. Halfway through, though, I waved my arm to gesture to a feature of the house, and I heard a sickening crack. I'd knocked the chimney off. For a second, everyone froze, and then, you will never believe this: *Olivia Allen* jumped up and quickly reattached it while I continued my presentation! Mrs. Carr smiled approvingly at Olivia as she worked. She was kind of pasting it with some extra frosting, and once it was back on, she took her seat until I finished. At the end I said, "And a special thanks to everyone who helped me on the house: my granddad, my friends at the Cupcake Club, Matt Taylor, and . . . Olivia Allen for saving the chimney, which was a huge part of Victorian life." She nodded in acknowledgment while everyone applauded and I bowed. It was a major triumph, in a lot of ways.

George Martinez called out, "Can we eat it now?" Everyone laughed while Mrs. Carr threatened them all with a trip to the principal's office if they so much as touched it, but I didn't care. I even considered saying yes, but I figured the feeding frenzy that would result would ruin everyone else's presentations.

That afternoon we all gathered at Katie's to do our weekend baking. I was feeling so relaxed, with everything resolved with Olivia, my project finished and turned in, and a handful of fun surprises lined up for my mom's birthday.

I did Mona's minis today, since Emma wanted to work on some of the new recipes—the strawberry shortcakes and the apple-cinnamon cupcakes in particular. Mia fried the bacon, and Katie colored the pink frosting for the ballerina cupcakes, and we were like an efficient, well-oiled machine.

"We've really got the assembly-line thing down!" I said later as we stood in a row frosting cupcakes at the counter. "Henry Ford would be proud!"

"Why? Who's he?" asked Katie.

"The car guy who invented the assembly line!" I said.

"Hey, I've been meaning to ask you. Whatever happened with Olivia?" asked Mia.

"Yeah!" agreed Katie. "We never heard another peep from you about it."

I hesitated, tempted to tell them the whole story, but then I decided to be a duck and let it roll off my back. "You know, I think we buried the hatchet," I said, shrugging casually.

"How?" asked Emma.

"We acted like ducks!" I said, and then I laughed maniacally.

Everyone started quacking, and that was the end of the discussion.

Early Saturday morning I went with Emma to deliver the mini cupcakes to Mona and then the apple-cinnamon ones to the baby shower for Jake's old teacher. Emma came home with me afterward to help set up the little birthday lunch my dad was organizing for my mom. The Taylors would be coming later (hopefully with Matt, but he might have a game), and two of Mom's other good friends and their families, and my grandparents, of course.

Dylan had bought a really cute pink tablecloth and napkins and party plates with a ballerina theme, and she was making her specialty: tea sandwiches (four kinds: turkey, cucumber, egg salad, and tomato), and we'd have iced tea and coffee and chips, and then the cupcakes. It was going to be great!

My dad had just returned from the framer's when we walked in. "Oh good! I was just going to wrap these, but now you can see them first. Look!" He was really pleased, I could tell.

He pulled two large matching picture frames out of a shopping bag. The first one had my mom's yellow gingham dress with the pear on it, framed in a pretty yellow wooden shadowbox. It was cute and cheerful. In the lower right corner of the frame was the photo of my mom in the dress, all cute and scraggly and messy. The second frame was pink, of course, and had a pink tulle ballet skirt of my mom's that my grandma had also found, with the ballerina picture of my mom in the lower right corner. The two framed items made a pretty matched set. My dad planned to move some things around, so we could hang them in our den, above the sofa.

I hugged him. "Oh, Dad! They look amazing! She'll love them!"

"And the dollhouse!" he said.

"And the dollhouse!" I agreed.

"I also got her a little charm for her charm bracelet," he said with a mischievous grin.

"Cute! What is it?" I asked.

But he wagged his finger at me. "You'll have to wait and see!"

❀

At the party, my mom had a great time. She loved all the pink decorations and the food, and the dollhouse was a huge hit with everyone! My dad had set it up in the living room for the party, and my mom was so surprised when she saw it. I personally couldn't wait to spend some time on it with her; one thing I wanted to find was a platter of tiny cupcakes for the little kitchen.

Speaking of cupcakes, when I explained to her the different kinds of cupcakes we'd made for the party and how they represented different parts of her life, she gave me a huge hug and got a little teary.

"Alexis, you are so special. Thank you for your thoughtfulness. I never knew you had such an interest in my past!"

"Neither did I!" I said. "Maybe it's just something you have to grow into."

When my dad presented her with the tiny jewelry box that I knew contained a charm, I held my breath. She unwrapped the tissue and opened the little velvet pouch, and in it was a gold . . . duck!

She and I laughed so hard, and we knew it was just the perfect thing. In fact, I couldn't believe she didn't already have one!

Dylan looked at us like we were cuckoo, but I didn't care since that was nothing new.

"Great job, Dad!" I said, and he beamed with pride.

Later that afternoon, Mia and Katie came over and, along with Emma, we worked on our time capsule and ate leftovers from the party.

We laid out everything to photograph, and I also went and photographed the framed items of my mom's.

It was fun to see what people had brought. Mia had some old costumes of her mom's from her wardrobe days, plus some crazy bell-bottomed pants she used to wear, and an exotic feather hat. Emma had an old book of her mom's that had stories she'd handwritten into it when she was a little girl, and Katie had a skateboard that had been her mom's! I couldn't even picture her mom riding it, but Katie said she was actually pretty decent at it. Katie also had the photo of her and Callie. I didn't say anything, because I didn't want to draw attention to it, but I was proud of her for including it.

Everyone passed around their biographies, and we read them. Then we loaded up the capsule, which was really a plastic Tupperware sandwich holder Mia had gotten from her mom. Then we put it into a giant Ziploc bag, and another and another and another! It seemed pretty watertight. I had received permission from my dad to bury it in a corner of the yard, under the magnolia tree, and that was where we headed now, armed with a big shovel.

We took turns digging, and when the hole was ready, Mia did the honors of placing the capsule into the hole.

"It feels like we're having a funeral!" remarked Emma.

"A funeral for our past," said Katie.

"Here's to the future!" I cried.

"Hooray!" we all said.

That night, my mom came to tuck me in.

"That was a great birthday, thanks to your thoughtfulness, sweetheart."

I snuggled happily under my covers. "It was fun."

"Your gingerbread house was wonderful too. You've had a very busy couple of days! But so many fun things!"

"I know."

"Now I hate to ask, but whatever happened

with Olivia at school? I kept waiting for you to mention it, so I didn't bring it up."

"Oh. Well . . . we've made peace," I said. "For now, anyway."

"Great! I'm so happy to hear that."

We smiled in the semidark for a minute, and then I said, "Mom, you know what? If you were a kid, we'd be best friends."

"Oh, Lexi! That's the best birthday present anyone could have ever given me! Thank you, sweetheart!" And she gave me a big squeeze.

I squeezed back and very softly, into her ear, I whispered, "Quack!"

Want another sweet cupcake?

Here's a sneak peek
of the thirteenth book in the

CUPCAKE  DIARIES

series:

Katie's
perfect
recipe

It's a Cupcake Code Red!

"Make me a doggy! Make me a doggy!"

I started to sweat as the adorable five-year-old in front of me looked up with pleading eyes. I knelt down and waved a round helium balloon in front of his face.

"It's not the kind of balloon that you can make into animals," I said, using my sweetest voice. "It's just a regular, fun, yellow balloon, to match the cupcakes! See?"

I pointed to the cupcake table across the small yard, where my friends Alexis and Emma were busy placing dozens of yellow and green cupcakes on matching paper plates.

The little boy's lower lip quivered. "But . . . I . . . want . . . a . . . doggy!" Then he began to bawl.

Panicked, I turned to my best friend, Mia, who was filling balloons behind me.

"Mia! We've got a code red!" I cried.

"Katie, what's wrong?" Mia asked.

I pointed to the sobbing boy. "He wants a dog-shaped balloon. I don't know what to do."

Mia quickly retrieved a black marker from her bag under a table and took the balloon from my hand. The marker squeaked as she drew a cute doggy face on the balloon, complete with droopy ears and a tongue sticking out. Thank goodness for a friend who can draw!

She handed it to the boy. "How's this?" she asked.

The boy stopped crying. "It's a doggy! Woof! Woof!" Happy again, he ran off.

I let out a sigh. "Mia to the rescue! Thank you. I knew this wasn't going to be easy. Running a party for a bunch of five-year-olds? It's much easier when we bake the cupcakes, serve the cupcakes, and then get out."

A while ago, my friends and I had started a Cupcake Club. We'd turned it into a pretty successful business, baking cupcakes for all kinds of parties and events.

"It's just like Alexis said, it's healthy to branch out," Mia pointed out. "We're making a lot more money by running the games and activities."

I gazed around the yard. We had worked hard on this cupcake-themed party for a five-year-old girl named Madison. Last night we were up late baking cupcakes in Madison's favorite colors, yellow and green. This morning we got up early (which I never like to do on a Saturday) to set things up. We had a table where the kids could decorate their own cupcakes.

Later, we were going to set up the stuff for the games. We took regular party games and cupcaketized them. You know, instead of Hot Potato, we were going to play Pass the Cupcake. And instead of a donkey, kids could pin a cherry on top of a giant picture of a cupcake. It was going to be fun, but it was definitely a lot of work.

"Well, money isn't everything," I declared. "If Alexis wants us to do this stuff so bad, she can come over here and make balloons. I'm going to go work at the cupcake table. At least I know what I'm doing there."

"Aw, come on, Katie, balloons are fun!" Mia said, bopping me over the head with a green one.

I stuck my tongue out at her. "But crying kids are not! I'll see you later."

I walked over to the cupcake-decorating table.

"Alexis, you need to switch with me," I said. "I can't do the balloons. I just don't have it in me."

Alexis nodded, her wavy red hair bouncing on her shoulders. "No problem. There's not much more setting up to do. Mrs. Delfino said that the kids are having pizza in a minute, and then we're going to play some games before we do the cupcake thing."

Alexis walked away, and I took her place behind the table, next to Emma, who really loves dressing up for any event. She wore a light yellow shirt with a short green skirt that matched the cupcakes perfectly. A yellow headband with tiny green flowers held back her straight, blond hair. I had tried to get in the party spirit too, with a yellow T-shirt and green sneakers.

"Katie, you look miserable!" Emma said. "Come on, it's not so bad, is it?"

"I think it's because I'm an only child," I admitted. "I don't know how to deal with little kids."

"That's not true. You're so great with Jake," Emma said. Jake is her six-year-old brother. "He adores you!"

"That's different," I protested. "Jake is only one kid. This is, like, a hundred!"

Emma laughed. "It's only sixteen. But I know

what you mean. When Jake's friends are over, it can be too much sometimes."

As we spoke, a woman with curly brown hair stepped into the yard.

"Okay, everybody! It's pizza time! Everyone inside!"

The kids cheered and raced inside, accompanied by the moms who had decided to stay for the party. Alexis approached the cupcake table.

"We should set up the games while everyone eats," she suggested. "Then we'll be ready when they come back out."

"Good idea," Emma agreed. We started to set things up for the games, and after only about ten minutes, the kids came racing back outside.

I shook my head. "Back already? What did they drink with their pizza? Rocket fuel?"

"Games! Games! Games!" the kids started chanting.

Mrs. Delfino smiled at us apologetically. "I hope you don't mind."

"Of course not," Alexis said crisply. When she's on a job, she's all business. "We're ready."

"Come on, kids!" Emma said loudly. "Who wants to play Pass the Cupcake?"

Sixteen hands flew into the air at once. "Meeeee!"

I kind of got into it when we played the games. We played Pass the Cupcake first. Mia had sewn a cute cupcake out of felt, and the kids sat in a circle and passed it around when the music played. When the music stopped, the kid holding the cupcake had to leave the circle.

It went pretty well until one little girl started crying when she got out. I almost panicked again. But then I had an idea. I grabbed the girl's hands.

"Everybody outside the circle gets to dance!" I cried, and then I started to dance and twirl around with her. It worked! She stopped crying, and soon all the kids outside the circle were laughing and dancing.

After that, we played Pin the Cherry on the Cupcake using a beautiful poster of a cupcake Mia had drawn, and big cherries cut out of paper. Then we did cupcake relay races, where the runners had to balance a cupcake on the end of a spatula while they were running (instead of the usual egg on a spoon). There was a lot of icing on the grass, but the kids seemed to really like it.

"Great job, everybody!" Alexis called out. "And now it's time to decorate cupcakes. Madison, since you're the birthday girl, you get to go first."

"Yay!" Madison's big brown eyes shone with

excitement as she ran to the cupcake table. Her party guests were excited too, and they quickly crowded around her.

"One at a time! One at a time!" Alexis yelled, but the five-year-olds ignored her, swarming around the table and grabbing the cupcakes, sprinkles, and candy toppings.

"Hey! There are spoons for that!" Alexis scolded.

Mia, Emma, and I quickly jumped in to help. I picked up a spoon and tried to show one blond-haired boy how to gently sprinkle some edible green glitter on to his cupcake. He took the spoon from me, dipped it in the glitter . . . and then threw the glitter all over the little girl next to him!

The girl looked stunned. She brushed the green glitter off her face . . . and then started to cry.

"Oh no. Not again," I said, moaning. I didn't think dancing was going to help this one. "We've got another code red!"

But everyone was too busy to come to my rescue. Emma was wiping off frosting from Madison's face, Mia was patiently creating a smiley face made out of candies on another girl's cupcake, and Alexis was marching up and down the table, trying to regain order.

"Icing goes on the cupcake, not on your

hands!" she shouted. "And, Leonard, do not put the sprinkle spoon in your mouth!"

Within minutes, the kids were more decorated than the cupcakes.

Mrs. Delfino approached the table, looking flustered. "Oh dear! This is quite a mess!"

We stopped and looked at one another. Our client did not look happy—and that was bad for business.

"It's, um, all part of the fun," I said cheerfully. "And don't worry, we'll clean it up. Who wants to play the Clean-Up Game?"

Sixteen sticky hands flew in the air. "Meeeeeeee!"

Luckily, Emma had thought to pack a big tub of wet wipes. I got out the box and gave one to each kid.

"Okay, now it's time to clean our hands, hands, hands," I instructed in a singsong voice, and luckily, the kids all played along. Next, I had them clean their faces, elbows, and even their knees (that's how messy everyone was!). In the end we had one big pile of messy wet wipes and one yard full of clean kids.

"It's time to sing the birthday song!" Mrs. Delfino announced, and as the kids followed her inside, we collapsed on the grassy lawn, exhausted.

"Katie, you were so good with the kids!" Mia said.

"Yeah, I'll have to remember that clean-up game for Jake," Emma said.

I frowned. "Well, thanks, but that was still awful. Doesn't this prove we should stick to just cupcakes from now on?"

"Absolutely not," Alexis said. "It just means we need to perfect our plan. Until that big cupcake mess, everything was going really well."

"Yeah." Mia nodded in agreement. "It was kind of fun, too."

"Definitely," said Emma. "And let's not forget the extra money. It's worth it."

I sighed. "I guess you're right. You know me. I don't really like changing the way I do things. In fifth grade, I wore the same pair of purple sneakers every day for a year. My mother said she had to peel them off my feet, literally."

Everyone laughed.

"Don't worry, Katie," Alexis said. "Our new business plan is going to be great. You'll see."

"Fine," I said. "But next time, let's leave the icing *on* the cupcakes, okay?"

Want more

CUPCAKE🧁DIARIES?

Visit **CupcakeDiariesBooks.com**
for the series trailer, excerpts, activities,
and everything you need for throwing
your own cupcake party!

How well do you know the Cupcake girls?

Take our quiz and find out!

(If you don't want to write in your book, use a separate piece of paper.)

1. Emma has three brothers. What are their names?

   A. Joe, Mark, and Sam

   B. Matt, Sam, and John

   C. Jake, Matt, and Sam

   D. Tom, Dick, and Harry

2. Who *loves* to dance?

   A. Mia

   B. Alexis

   C. Emma

   D. Katie

3. What unusual ingredient do the girls use in one of their most popular cupcakes?

> **A.** Salami
>
> **B.** French fries
>
> **C.** Bacon
>
> **D.** Pizza

yum!

4. Where does Emma model?

> **A.** At the summer day camp
>
> **B.** At The Special Day wedding salon
>
> **C.** At the local swimming pool
>
> **D.** At school dances

5. Mia has a BFF in New York whose first name has three letters too. What is her friend's name?

> **A.** Amy
>
> **B.** Gia
>
> **C.** Ava
>
> **D.** Ivy

6. George teases Katie and calls her a funny nickname. (But it's okay though because Katie knows he likes her.) What is the nickname?

A. Chicken Legs

B. Silly Arms

C. Bigfoot

D. Man Hands

7. Which Cupcake girl has curly red hair?

A. Alexis

B. Mia

C. Katie

D. Emma

8. Who is the "mean girl" who loves to torture the Cupcake girls?

A. Sydney

B. Beth

C. Olivia

D. Both A and C

Did you get the right answers?

1. C   5. C
2. B   6. B
3. C   7. A
4. B   8. D

What your answers mean:

If you got all 8 answers right:
Wow! You know your Cupcake girls.
Four cupcakes for you!

If you got 6 to 7 answers right:
Pretty good! You just need to brush up a little bit on
your four Cupcake friends. Two cupcakes for you!

If you got 4 to 5 answers right:
You need to reread your favorite Cupcake books, but
you get one cupcake for your efforts!

If you got less than four answers right:
You're not paying attention. Reread this book (and all
your favorite Cupcake books) right now! No cupcake
for you—have a cookie!

Coco Simon always dreamed of opening a cupcake bakery but was afraid she would eat all of the profits. When she's not daydreaming about cupcakes, Coco edits children's books and has written close to one hundred books for children, tweens, and young adults, which is a lot less than the number of cupcakes she's eaten. Cupcake Diaries is the first time Coco has mixed her love of cupcakes with writing.

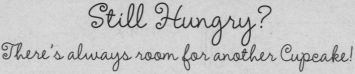

Still Hungry?

There's always room for another Cupcake!

Katie and the Cupcake Cure

978-1-4424-2275-9 $5.99
978-1-4424-2276-6 (eBook)

Mia in the Mix

978-1-4424-2277-3 $5.99
978-1-4424-2278-0 (eBook)

Emma on Thin Icing

978-1-4424-2279-7 $5.99
978-1-4424-2280-3 (eBook)

Alexis and the Perfect Recipe

978-1-4424-2901-7 $5.99
978-1-4424-2902-4 (eBook)

Katie, Batter Up!

978-1-4424-4611-3 $5.99
978-1-4424-4612-0 (eBook)

Mia's Baker's Dozen

978-1-4424-4613-7 $5.99
978-1-4424-4614-4 (eBook)

Emma All Stirred Up!
978-1-4424-5078-3 $5.99
978-1-4424-5079-0 (eBook)

Alexis Cool as a Cupcake
978-1-4424-5080-6 $5.99
978-1-4424-5081-3 (eBook)

Katie and the Cupcake War
978-1-4424-5373-9 $5.99
978-1-4424-5374-6 (eBook)

Mia's Boiling Point
978-1-4424-5396-8 $5.99
978-1-4424-5397-5 (eBook)

Emma, Smile and Say "Cupcake!"
978-1-4424-5398-2 $5.99
978-1-4424-5400-2 (eBook)

Alexis Gets Frosted
978-1-4424-6867-2 $5.99
978-1-4424-6868-9 (eBook)

Katie's New Recipe
978-1-4424-7168-9 $5.99
978-1-4424-7169-6 (eBook)

If you liked

cupcake  DIARIES

be sure to check out these

other series from

Simon Spotlight

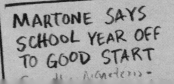
MARTONE SAYS
SCHOOL YEAR OFF
TO GOOD START